Terror Town

Young Pete Henderson and his mentor Hank McDonald
were like tumbleweed, never staying in one place and
forever riding and working and then riding again. On this
occasion though, they stumbled upon a murdered
prospector near the Arizona badlands and found an official claim to a goldmine – or rather half of one.

The pair duly reported the death to the sheriff of notorious Diablo – the nearest town, haunt of some of the
worst scum of the territory. From that moment on their
lives were in constant danger and only their formidable
skills with fists and guns kept them from Boot Hill.

But could they solve the murder and capture those who
sought to kill them? There were many battles to be fough
and surprises to be encountered in that hell-hole calle
Diablo which was indeed a Terror Town.

Terror Town

AL BRADY

A Black Horse Western

ROBERT HALE · LONDON

© 1950, 2003 Vic J. Hanson.
First hardcover edition 2003
Originally published in paperback as
Terror Town by V. Joseph Hanson

ISBN 0 7090 7259 7

Robert Hale Limited
Clerkenwell House
Clerkenwell Green
London EC1R 0HT

Typeset by
Derek Doyle & Associates, Liverpool.
Printed and bound in Great Britain by
Antony Rowe Limited, Wiltshire.

PROLOGUE

San Diablo Creek was its name. 'Diablo' for short or, if like the fabulous old-timers who built it, you had a taste for the flamboyant, 'The Devil's Frying Pan.' It had been a boom-town, a gold-town. The creek running down from the hills brought a stream of wealth. The small ranches went to seed while their owners took up something that showed far more profit; and from all over the West gold-seekers came to scratch and sift, and squabble. On top of them all came the badmen, the gamblers, the women, the parasites of both sexes. Diablo began to rival Tombstone and Julesburg in vice, and present a quota of killings that was quite in the tradition.

Lawmen came and went. The lucky ones on galloping nags, the others in long boxes or sewn up in blankets like sides of pork. A few of them were buried in the Boot Hill cemetery that spread rapidly like a loathsome rash behind the town.

For two gory, glorious years Diablo boomed, sweating in blood and heat, living up to its title of 'The Devil's Frying Pan.' Then gradually the golden stream petered out, the bottom of the creek became all mud once more; despite frantic blasting operations the hills refused to shower any more wealth on their violators. The Mexicans said that, like women, the hills had for a while been attracted by the lust, but now they were tired and stubborn. They laid a black curse upon their tormentors and frowned upon the town these squabbling humans had spawned.

The gringoes went back to their ranches and farms, the Mexicans and Indians to their fastnesses behind the hills or over the border. Most of the genuine prospectors made tracks for richer fields. But it seemed that the hills had indeed laid a curse on Diablo for, because of its easy accessibility to the border, it became the rendezvous of outlaws with money to spend and gamble, and unbridled lusts to satiate. And the girls and the gamblers stayed.

Wanderers coming upon the town suddenly in the hot wastelands were surprised to learn that it was the notorious hellspot they had heard so much about. On the surface it was just like any other sordid mushroom town, lethargic, smelly and dusty by day. But it was at night that Diablo really began to sing.

A wanderer did not have to sojourn there for long before the subtle evil of the place began to grip him. It was a bad place. Its bad people outnumbered the good by three to one.

But the vice of Diablo was well-organised. The town kept an outward aura of respectability; its killings were concealed or made legal. U.S. marshals came and went, finding nothing. Diablo earned immunity from a clean-up such as had visited many of its contemporaries as the law marched across the frontier.

ONE

The elder of the two was thin almost to the point of emaciation, big-boned like the grey mare he strode. His face was the colour and texture of leather that had been drying in the sun a long time; wrinkled and immobile, enlivened only by cold, alert grey eyes.

His partner was easily thirty years his junior; a young man of twenty odd summers, flashily yet nonchalantly dressed; dark, devil-may-care, riding a spirited-looking black gelding.

Since young Pete Henderson's parents had been killed in a prairie-fire, his pa's best friend Hank McDonald, had been Pete's guardian. Now the younker was over twenty-one; he had proved himself, years ago, a worthy partner to grim old Hank. They made a striking picture riding together…. flint and steel!

Old Hank carried a bitterness in his soul that twenty odd years had not served to erase. When he was about Pete's age he had laid his heart at the feet of a prairie belle. Miraculously enough, out of all her suitors she had chosen him. They had married in the fulness of a Western summer and spent a few years of passion and idyllic happiness. Hank had worked and saved, his great love blinding him to his wife's now too obvious shortcomings; her fond-

7

ness for unattached young men – even for the husbands of her neighbours. He saved enough to realise his ambition and buy a little spread of his own. But the humdrum life of a small rancher's wife did not suit Stella, the prairie belle. They had been married five years when she ran away with a gambler whom she had met on a trip to San Antonio.

For two days Hank roamed around his small-holdings in a grief-stricken stupor, hoping maybe it was all a dream, and he would wake up sometime. Then on the third morning he awoke from a sleep of exhaustion to the full realisation of his soul-searing unhappiness. And with it was an overmastering hate of the man who had caused it: the suave gambler who had taken his wife away from him.

He paid off his two hands, buckled on his gunbelt and, taking his horse, rifle, and a roll of money, set out. He resolved not to stop riding until he had caught up with the runaways and killed the gambler.

A six-months' trail led him finally to Dodge City where he discovered the gambler had been killed in a gaming dispute and Stella was living with a rich saloon-owner. Even so he sought her out. But when he found her she turned on him like a tigress, asked him how he dared follow her, told him she wanted no more truck with saddle-tramps. Only then did he realise how irrevocably she was lost to him.

He left Dodge City quietly, a bitter man, old beyond his years, caring not whether he lived or died.

For years he roamed from end to end of the West, working as a cowpuncher on ranches, and now and then trying his luck in the towns, striving to lose himself in gambling or the company of dance-hall women.

Then he met up with old 'Curly' Henderson, Pete's father, who gave him a job on his small ranch. Hank liked this bluff, frizzy-haired old rancher; he stayed with him longer than was his wont. He stayed there over a year before the old ache returned as unbearably as before, and he felt compelled to move on. Old 'Curly' told him that if ever he felt like coming back there would be a job for him. Within eighteen months he had returned.

Four times he did this. Each time his period of absence was shorter. The fourth time he returned old 'Curly' tried a shot in the dark and made him foreman of his steadily growing ranch.

He was there when the terrible fire ravaged the range and burnt Henderson's ranch to the ground. Hank and young Pete escaped with minor injuries. Pete's mother was trapped in the house and killed by a falling beam. Old 'Curly' went in to find her and was badly burnt himself. He died two days later, making Hank promise he would care for young Pete before he did so.

Hank kept his promise faithfully. After the funeral the man and the youth rode away from the heaps of ashes that had been their home. They had been riding ever since. Riding, and working, and riding again. They had been in tight corners together and in some parts of the West their presence had left behind the echoes of a legend, to be repeated and magnified by the lips of garrulous old-timers.

Young Pete wished for no other life and, as for grim old Hank, maybe in his heart of hearts he was happier now than he had been since the wreckage of his ill-fated marriage. To him now women were non-existent – and gamblers were pizen!

The mid-day sun beat down on them, on their dusty clothes, on the stocks of the rifles on their saddle-horns; making them too hot to touch. The territory they traversed could hardly have been called range land. The grass, yellow and brittle, was burnt down close to the ground. There was no vegetation except for a few parched, stunted cacti. The ground was bumpy and hillocky, but they could see for miles ahead: right out to where the shimmering, heat-haze obscured the horizon. They were on the outskirts of the Arizona 'badlands.'

Pete Henderson reached under the folded slicker on his saddle-horn and brought forth a water-canteen.

Hank McDonald turned his head. 'Don't drink too much, Pete,' he advised. 'We don't know how far the next water-hole is.' His voice was hoarse; the vocal sounds came slowly and laboriously from his parched larynx.

Pete returned the canteen to its place. 'We could turn back,' he said.

'Why.... d'yuh want to?'

'Do you?'

'Cain't say I do,' said Hank slowly. 'I've never bin in this neck o' the woods before.'

'Nor me,' said Pete. He grinned: a flash of white teeth in his sun-browned face. 'I guess that's enough for us ain't it, pardner?'

'Yeh.... I guess it is.'

The heat-haze receded as they moved forward, and pretty soon they could dimly see, blue and fluctuating in the distance, a line of hills.

'That'll be the Aurora foothills,' said Hank. 'We oughta be purty close to 'em come sundown.'

'Water there I reckon,' said Pete.

'I reckon.'

Sure enough they had very much shortened the distance by sundown. The foothills, tinted now by the rosy light of the setting sun, looked almost close enough to touch. The ground was becoming jagged and uneven, and bestrewn with outcrops of rock.

Night fell swiftly, dark, moonless, the stars too high to give much light. Rather than struggle on, risking their horses' limbs on the uneven ground in the blackness, the two men decided to camp beneath a particularly huge outcrop of rock. It had a hollow at its base plenty large enough for both of them, and its bulk would protect them from the night-winds.

They set the horses to graze with a nose-bag each and, with a bundle of sticks that Hank had very providently gathered before they hit the 'badlands' proper, they lit a small fire, keeping it going with small tufts of dry, brown grass and cactus-stalks. Over this they hotted a tin of beans and brewed coffee – a meagre half-cupful each.

They were both awake at dawn and saddled their horses right away. They set off without breakfast, hoping they would find a water-hole or spring before long.

'I guess there must be water up here someplace,' said Pete.

Hardly were the words out of his mouth when the first howl startled them.

'A coyote!'

'That's never a coyote,' said Hank. 'More like a wolf or a dog.'

The howl came again, eerie, drawn-out, agonising.

Simultaneously both men spurred their horses to a trot. They were instinctive actions born of their insatiable curiosity. They were at the edge of the foothills now, at the base of a small hill. It was from behind this the howl seemed to come. It came again....

'That's a dog,' said Hank.

Pete shivered as he eased his horse gently up the slippery hill. That howl seemed a sound of the night rather than the early morning. Hearing it now made it seem more sinister. Portentous....

They were at the top of the hill now, looking down at the roof of a log cabin in the little green valley below. A huge sycamore bent its boughs over the house. Not many yards from the door ran a narrow, clear stream. Beside the stream sat a huge husky and, as the men watched, he lifted his muzzle and howled once more.

'Sump'n's wrong here,' said Hank, spurring his horse down the slope. Pete followed him.

The dog became aware of their presence and rose to its legs, facing them challengingly, its cry changing to a deep-chested growl. It was a magnificent-looking beast: a pure-bred, powerful, fighting husky.

It crouched, showing its white fangs as the two men, with Hank in the forefront, came nearer. Then, as Hank's mare put its first hoof in the shallow stream the dog sprang.

Hank swerved his horse with an instinctive pressure of his knees, drawing his gun in one swift movement. As the dog hurtled past in mid-air he brought the gun-barrel down on its head. The dog hit the ground in a heap, rolled over, then lay still.

Hank dismounted and bent over the beast. Pete joined him.

'I've only stunned him,' said the older man. 'He'll be all right.'

'He's a lovely beast,' said Pete.

'Yeh,' said Hank. He was already remounting and easing his mare thru' the shallow stream. Pete caught up with him outside the door of the cabin. Both men dismounted again.

The cabin door was shut. The place was silent; no smoke came from the squat, blackened brick chimney.

Hank lifted the door latch and pushed. The door opened inwards with a quietly protesting squeak. As it did so Hank instinctively drew his gun.

Both men stared into the shadowy interior of the hut lit only by the light of the small window beside the door. Gradually their eyes became accustomed to the half-light, and they distinguished the shape of different objects: the bunk, with tumbled blankets, against the opposite wall; the table in the middle of the floor; two chairs, a packing case... The two men stepped into the room.

Hank halted, his gun pointed across the table at a dark bundle on the floor beside the bunk. But he lowered his gun. It was not another dog – but a man. Hank skirted the table in a few swift strides and dropped on one knee beside the prostrate form.

Pete joined him and they looked down at the grey, grizzled head of an old man. Gently Hank turned him over.

On the breast of the faded shirt {the old man wore only shirt and trousers, and was barefoot} was a spreading red stain.

Hank bent closer.

'He's dead all right,' he said. 'But I don't think he's bin dead long.'

Pete started forward and, reaching under the bunk drew forth a sawed-off shotgun. He broke it.

'It's loaded,' he said. 'But it ain't been fired.'

'So most likely the old guy was murdered.'

'That looks about the size of it.' Pete was rummaging under the bunk again. He brought forth a shallow metal pan: a gold prospector's pan. It was black at the edges but the bottom was shiny, scratched and scoured.

'It's purty evident what the old man was doin' up here all on his lonesome,' he said.

'Yeh.... There's probably gold somewhere in these hills,' said Hank. 'Mebbe somewhere along that little crick outside.' He got up and began to prowl around the little cabin.

A sharp exclamation brought Pete to his side. Hank was looking down at the floor beneath the window. A floorboard had been ripped up and carelessly replaced so that a gap showed. They could see the black earth beneath in a shaft of sunlight that slanted thru' the window.

Hank bent and lifted the floorboard. The ground immediately beneath was bare, but disturbed, as if it had been scratched by searching fingers. Hank got down on his knees and wormed his hand underneath the adjoining boards.

'Ah!' he said. He brought forth an old hide 'war-bag.'

Pete leaned forward eagerly as the older man put his hand inside.

'Empty.' Hank turned it upside down and shook it.

A minute quantity of fine, golden dust sprinkled their feet.

'This was the old guy's cache shore 'nough' said Hank. 'This was what he was murdered for.'

'He was asking for it livin' up here on his lonesome,' said Pete.

'Mebbe he had a pardner an' the pardner killed him.'

'Wal, the pardner didn't live here that's evident. There's barely room for one man on that bunk. An' there's no sign of anybody else a-sleeping here.' Pete was looking around on the floor as he spoke. He gave an exclamation and picked something up from behind a leg of the table. It sparkled in his hand as the sunlight caught it.

'You know what this is, don't yuh?'

'Yeh – It's a spike of one o' them fancy Mexican rowels.'

'That's somep'n the old guy here wouldn't wear, so we can safely assume it belonged to his killer.'

Hank looked reflective. Then he said: 'Mebbe he used his heel and his spur to prise this floorboard up.' He illustrated his point with his own ordinary steel spur.... 'Or mebbe it was already damaged and he jest happened to drop it here.'

'He couldn't 'uv noticed it anyway.' Pete dropped the small glittering spike into a pocket of his black, embroidered vest.

They searched the hut a bit longer, trying not to disturb anything more than was necessary. They found nothing else of interest until Pete took a small photograph from the top of the row of shelves where the old prospector had kept his little necessities. The wooden frame was patently home-made and the glass was grimy and cracked in one corner. The photo was of a girl, looking to be about sixteen or seventeen, with a cloud of dark hair, big dark eyes and a shy smile. At the bottom of the photo was scrawled, in a round childish hand: *To Dad with love from Ella.* Beneath this was a row of kisses.

'The old guy's daughter I guess,' said Pete. He turned the photo over. It was backed by a strip of plywood held in place by two bent nails. Pete straightened the nails with his thumb and lifted the wood. There was a folded piece of dirty paper beneath it.

Hank watched him closely as he unfolded it.

'It's an official claim for a gold-mine,' said Pete. 'Or at least half of one.'

He handed the paper to Hank.

'There's a half of a name on it – Joseph T.... somebody.'

'It's funny the murderer never looked for this.'

'Mebbe he did.... Mebbe we disturbed him – or the dog did.'

'Mebbe he got the other half anyway,' said Hank. 'It's an old dodge of prospectors to keep one half of their claim on them and the other half hidden someplace.' He gave the paper back to Pete. 'Mebbe you'd better put it in your vest pocket with that rowel.'

Pete grinned wryly. 'I'd better have the picture complete,' he said. He replaced the paper in its hiding-place and put the little photo in his pocket. Hank watched him with a quizzical look in his cold grey eyes, but he did not say anything.

'There isn't much more we can do here, now,' said Pete.

'No,' agreed Hank. 'The best thing we can do is find the nearest sheriff or marshal, and report this.'

As he stepped outside something buzzed by him like an angry hornet. The flat echoes of a rifle shot came from the hills. Something plucked at Pete's shirt on the shoulder. Both men dodged back into the hut.

'Whoever it is he was too eager,' said Hank.

'It seemed to come from at the side there,' said Pete. He gestured with his hand. 'We shouldn't be able to see him from the window.'

'He's picked the spot well,' said Hank. 'There's no way we can get out without him seeing us.'

'Best thing to do is make a run for it. He won't be expecting that right away.'

Both men drew their guns.

They were halfway to their horses before the bushwhacker opened fire again. A slug whipped Hank's Stetson from his head. Hank retaliated, firing pretty vainly at a puff of smoke.

Then the bushwhacker stood up, exposing himself to get a better shot at the partners.

Pete reached his own horse first and lifted his rifle from the saddle-horn. Turning he saw the huge husky, whom they had left stunned, rising to his feet.

The dog saw the man up on the bluff and with a snarl ran towards him. With one parting shot, which kicked up the dust behind Pete the man disappeared. The dog climbed on up the slope to where he had stood. The partners mounted their horses and were not slow in following.

They reached the top of the bluff, beside the huge boulder behind which the man had hidden, and looked down at a trail which went off at right angles to the one along which they had come that morning.

'There were two men,' said Pete.

The husky was loping behind the riders and steadily gaining.

As Hank and Pete watched one of the men turned and raised a gun. The slug kicked up a spurt of dust just to the right of the dog.

The man fired again. The dog halted. Then he plunged on, but his pace was perceptibly slower.

'Looks like he's hit,' said Pete, as they spurred their horses down the slope.

The horseman turned and fired again. His companion turned also and followed suit. They poured a regular fusil-lade at the luckless beast.. He collapsed and rolled over. The horsemen holstered their guns and rode on at a faster pace.

'Poor beast,' said Pete as they drew level. 'He's a fighter. I guess he knows all right who murdered his master. It's a pity he can't talk.'

'He's dyin' fast,' said Hank, drawing his gun. He leaned over and put a bullet in the courageous animal's brain.

The killers had gotten too big a start. The partners lost them in another range of the foothills. Traversing these they saw, almost obscured by the afternoon heat-haze, a small town on the horizon.

'I guess that's the Diablo we've heard so much about,' said Hank.

'A fittin' place for them two killers to hole-up in.'

TWO

Dusk was falling as Hank McDonald and Pete Henderson, two men who knew their West and its many-sided facets too well, rode into 'The Devil's Frying-Pan.' Lights were flashing on in the numerous saloons, gambling-hells, dance-halls and brothels along its single main street.

The partners made for the biggest building: a garish place called the 'San Diablo Palace.' In the smaller type beneath the title were the words: 'Sam Fernicutt, Proprietor.'

'They've got their own livery-stable I see,' said Hank. He swerved his horse and made for the open double doors of the 'San Diablo Palace Livery Stable.' Pete read the title aloud. ''What a mouthful,' he said. 'This Sam Fernicutt shore seems to do things in style.'

A mournful individual, taller and more cadaverous even than Hank, took charge of their horses. He had been around horses so long he looked like one. Pete reflected they couldn't 've left their nags in better hands.

They swung thru' the batwings of the San Diablo Palace. The place was quiet as yet, altho' the bar was pretty busy. Over in a corner a fat man in a brilliant red shirt was tinkling desultorily on the drink-stained piano.

Hank and Pete took their stand at the end of the bar nearest the pianist and surveyed the room casually.

18

After a moment the bartender came to take their orders.

'Any strangers rode in here just lately?' Pete asked him.

The barman was unnaturally pallid and had a nervous twitch to his right eye. He looked at them suspiciously.

'There's strangers ridin' in here all the time,' he said huskily. 'An' it ain't safe to ask 'em questions.'

'I guess you're right, pardner,' said Pete affably. 'We're just after catchin' up with two buddies of ours, that's all.'

'Wal, I'm afraid I can't help you, gentlemen,' said the barman as he turned away.

'Close-mouthed cuss,' said Pete.

'Barmen in a place like this have to be close-mouthed,' Hank told him. 'It was a mistake really to draw his attention to us by asking him questions. Them hombres we're after might be regulars here. They might even be pals of his.'

'Mebbe you're right,' said Pete. 'They've got the advantage in any case. They can recognise us, whereas we didn't see them – or at least only a glimpse of one of 'em, and I'm durned sure I couldn't tell him again.'

'Same here.'

The barman returned with their drinks.

'You gents figgerin' on staying here?' he asked.

'Mebbe.... Where could we get a room?'

'There's one empty here if you want it,' the man told them.

The partners exchanged glances .'Can you show it to us now?' said Hank. 'If it's all right we'd like to dump our war-bags there.'

'Wal, I'm busy right now,' said the barman. 'But my pard 'ull take you up. If you like it will yuh come down again and register? I kin get you some supper too, if you want it.'

'We'll let you know.'

The barman's pardner turned out to be a thin, vicious-looking youth in a white apron. Without a word he led them up a wide flight of wooden stairs at the other end of the long bar.

They traversed a long landing laid with faded linoleum. Hank counted eight doors, four each side. Theirs turned out to be the end one which, with the one opposite, made ten all told.

'Quite a big place,' said Hank.

The vicious-looking youth flung open the door.

The room they found themselves in was clean if not elaborate. It had two large brass bedsteads, a table, a wash-stand and two chairs. The floor was bare boards covered on one side of each bed by a moth-eaten mat. The window was uncurtained.

The partners exchanged glances again.

Hank dumped his war-bag on the floor.

'We're not partic'lar,' he said. 'I guess this'll suit. You can vamoose, sonny. We'll be down a bit later on.'

The youth shot him a vicious glance and left, slamming the door behind him.

'I guess he didn't like bein' called sonny' said Hank, without the ghost of a smile. 'He thinks he's a badman.'

'Wal, if yore surmise is correct, old-timer, we're now right in the enemies' camp,' said Pete.

'Aw, I'm jest a suspicious ole cuss,' Hank told him. 'Them killers might be miles away by now…. Altho',' he added, 'I hope they ain't. I'd like to meet up with 'em sometime. I never did like bushwhackers – 'specially when they shoot at me.'

'D'yuh think we oughta report the murder to a law-officer right away?' Pete asked him.

'Might be the best thing to do. If we can find a law-officer in this town…. Anyway, I vote we go down pronto and look the place over. An' keep a lookout for a hombre with a spike missin' from his Mexican rowel.'

'You don't forgit anythin' do yuh?' said Pete as he followed him downstairs.

The barman smiled at them affably across the bar, giving his pallid face a sicklier tinge.

'He's thawin'-out,' whispered Pete.

'We'll take the room,' Hank told the barman.

'Wal, check in now if you like,' was his rejoinder. He produced a tattered register. The partners signed their names.

'How long you gents aiming to stop?' the barman asked them.

'Mebbe a night – mebbe two nights – mebbe a week,' said Hank airily.

'Well, if yuh're gonna pay nightly you pay in advance.'

'That'll suit us.'

Business satisfactorily concluded, Hank said: 'We're goin' to look the town over. We'll be back for supper.'

As they crossed the floor towards the batwings, out of the corner of his eye Pete saw the pimply-faced youth watching them malevolently. 'He looks a back-stabbiin' little cuss,' he reflected.

The night-life of Diablo was beginning to hum. As they passed down the dusty street people passing hither and thither brushed against them. Cowboys rode in from off the trail, curs yapped at the heels of their ponies. Saturnine Indians or half-breeds in serapes and high-crowned hats passed silently by. From the door of a shanty a blowsy, painted harlot called: 'You an' me, cowboy.'

'Wimmin,' ejaculated Hank, and he spat in the gutter.

Pete grinned and impetuously went over to the woman.

'Hey, what's the idea?' yelled Hank, starting after him.

'Is there a peace-officer in this town, *chiquita?*' Pete asked the woman.

'Yeh,' she said. 'Obadiah Withers, the marshal.' She

laughed shrilly: 'He don't bother me none tho'.'

'Where's he hang out?'

'He's got an office just down the street a piece,' said the woman. She leered at Pete. 'But a nice, handsome cowboy like you don't want to have no truck with no ole peace-officer. C'mon inside, honey.'

Pete pressed a coin into her palm. 'Not right now, *chiquita*,' he said. 'I gotta go now. Mebbe I'll see yuh later. Thanks for the information.'

'You're welcome, honey.' The hag simpered coyly. 'I'll be waitin' for yuh.'

Pete pulled a wry face as he turned back to Hank.

'You do the damndest things,' the older man burst out.

'I thought it 'ud be safer to ask her,' Pete told him. 'What say we go and see this marshal, Mr Obadiah Withers.'

'Could do,' said Hank.

They had no difficulty in finding the office. It was a drab little cabin with one window and 'Marshal' in dirty-white letters on the frame door. Beside it in contrast stood the new red-brick jail: so new it did not look as if it had ever been used. Probably it hadn't, Pete reflected wryly.

Hank was raising his fist to knock the door when things happened. Pete, half-turning, saw the two men in the dusk across the street draw their guns.

'Hank,' he yelled barging against his pard. Hank went sprawling, slugs whistling harmlessly over him and thudding into the marshal's door

Pete had drawn his gun and fired back. His first shot made one of the gunmen squeal with a smashed shoulder and drop his gun in the dust. Hank down on one knee, was triggering too. The other gunman dropped on his knees just in time to avoid having his face sliced in half by the old-timer's deadly 'fanning'.

His wounded companion turned and ran. The other

one rose to follow him and received two slugs close together plumb in his throat. He gave a choking scream and buckled up.

'You shore acted fast that time, Pete,' said Hank. 'I've got to hand it to yuh.'

'Jest Lady Luck I guess,' said Pete. 'I happened to turn and spot 'em. Another minute an' we'd 'uv both had our backs full of lead.'

The surrounding street, that had miraculously cleared, was beginning to fill up again. Folks came closer to the two men and the still form on the ground.

The door behind Hank and Pete squeaked as it opened. They turned to look into the wicked-looking muzzle of a sawed-off shotgun.

The weapon looked like a toy in the huge, flabby hands of the man who held it. He filled the doorway, stooping a little so that his hatless, bald head just missed the top. His faded check shirt bulged over the pin-striped store-trousers he wore tucked into dirty riding-boots. In the waist-band of the trousers was tucked a Derringer and a bowie-knife side by side. On the left-hand pocket of his shirt was a silver star.

The huge man's voice when he spoke was quite an ordinary one; it sounded almost incongruous coming from such a giant.

'Ah'm a peace-loving man mahself, but I simply will not tolerate people fillin' mah own office door with lead.' He jerked the gun in his hands. 'H'ist your hands, gentlemen.'

Hank and Pete complied. The latter grinned. 'Are you Marshal Obadiah Withers?' he asked.

'I am.'

'You're jest the man we want to see,' said Hank.

'You don't say,' said the marshal. His round, grey hairless face took on a look of cunning. His little eyes squinted in their flabby pouches of flesh.

'Wa-al,' he said slowly. 'Maybe Ah'd better ask you gentlemen inside…. But first of all fetch that carcass over here. Ah'll keep yuh covered jest in case.'

The two partners strode over to the body. 'Give 'em room,' called the marshal, making a sweeping movement with his shotgun. The crowd opened out.

Pete and Hank took a leg each of the fallen gunman, and dragging him across to the big man, dumped him at his feet.

'H-mm,' said the marshal. 'It's 'Jolly-boy' Cadman – no longer jolly. You made quite a mess of him. He's purty dead I guess.'

'Purty,' said Hank.

'Well – well,' said the marshal. 'He was a bad-hat. No loss to the community.' He raised his voice to address the crowd. 'Get this carrion out of the way some of yuh!'

Watching and listening to him Pete could not feel anything but admiration. It took guts to talk to the desperate dregs of the badlands in that manner.

The marshal motioned them inside, closing the door behind them.

'Take the two chairs against the wall,' he said.

He squeezed his own huge bulk into a swivel-chair behind a plain deal table which served as his desk, judging by the papers with which it was bestrewn. Thus he sat facing the two men, the shotgun on the desk in front of him, his finger very near the trigger, the muzzle pointing at them.

'Now,' he said.

Hank became spokesman and recounted to the marshal their adventures since they hit the foothills, carry-ing on right up to the incident that had just happened. He omitted, however, to tell the sheriff that Pete had half the old prospector's claim. He made no mention either of the broken rowel.

Pete smiled to himself. Canny old Mac. Incidentally, Pete had made sure the dead gunman outside had not worn Mexican rowels. In fact, he had not worn spurs at all.

While Hank was talking they heard scuffling outside and figured somebody was carrying out the marshal's orders and removing 'the carrion.'

'The old prospector is Joe Dempsey,' the marshal told the partners. 'Ah ain't surprised he got shot an' his cache was stolen— But Ah am surprised to learn he had struck lucky, everybody figured it had all petered out up there.... Evidently it didn't take somebody else long to get wise an' cash in on it – I allus told Joe he waz asking for trouble living up there all on his lonesome.... Wa-al, I guess Miss Stella 'ull have to be told....'

'Miss Stella!' echoed Pete. He saw his pard's face-muscles stiffen and remembered suddenly that Stella had been the name of Hank's faithless wife. He had known the whole tale a few years now – even since they had been real partners. He realised his thoughtless repetition of the name had reopened his pard's old wound.

'Miss Stella is old Joe's daughter,' explained Marshal Obadiah Withers. 'She keeps a little draper's shop down the street a piece.'

'A draper's shop?'

'Yes, a draper's shop,' repeated the marshal. 'The gels of the town want clothes an' hats, don't they? Miss Stella's no snob, altho' she's as pure as an angel herself.' The marshal's words and his indignation seemed so comic that Pete had difficulty in restraining a smile.

'Miss Stella has three Injuns workin' for her,' continued Withers. 'Two gels an' their ole pappy. The old man 'ud kill anybody who interfered with Miss Stella. An,' the marshal patted the stock of his shotgun, 'Ah'd be right behind him.'

'Don't she ever have trouble with the roughs?' asked

Pete, 'I guess hardly a day passes here without some lady-killin' desperado ridin' thru'.'

'Wal, it's like this,' explained Marshal Withers. 'There's three king-pins in this town. There's Sam Fernicutt, who owns the Diablo Palace an' the stables next to it. There's Ep Jackman who owns nearly all the rest of town 'cept this office an' the jail, an' Miss Stella's shop, which her pappy bought for her outright. An' there's Don Miguel Carmenito, and his son José, who've got a big hacienda and ranch on the edge of the border, but do some of their business in an office right here . . . Now Sam Fernicutt, Ep Jackman an' young José all want to marry Miss Stella. All three of 'em are crooks – you've got to be to live around here, but I must admit they've all played fair on this deal. Miss Stella wants no truck with either of 'em – Ah hate to think what 'ud happen if she was to pick any partic'ler one....'

For a moment Pete was tempted to show Withers the photo he had found in the prospector's cabin, but decided it was wiser to hold his hosses for the time being. He suddenly remembered the signature on the photo had been 'Ella.' Probably that had been the old man's nickname for his daughter. She'd be older now, but Pete guessed he would recognise her if he saw her.

The marshal was talking again. 'If any bozo interfered with Miss Stella an' the old Injun didn't get him, Fernicutt, Jackman or young José Carmenito would be shore to. Either them or one of the gunnies they employ. Between 'em they've got nearly everybody in Diablo on their payrolls. Ah daren't think what 'ud happen if they declared war on each other. Ah'm a peaceable man, I hate strife.' He patted his huge stomach. 'Sam Fernicutt's the straightest of the three, a man who'd never go back on his word. He's a personal friend o' mine.'

'We should like to meet him,' said Hank. 'We've got a

room at his place.'

Abruptly Marshal Withers changed the subject. He became strictly official again.

'D'yuh think the two who throwed down on yuh outside are the same two who killed old Joe?'

'Mebbe,' said Hank. 'As I told yuh, we didn't get a good look at 'em the first time.'

'Who did whats-is-name Cadman work for?' asked Pete.

'Oh, "Jolly-boy" Cadman.... Wal, I think he's worked in turn for all them Ah mentioned. Ah don't know who he wuz workin' for at present. Mebbe he wuz on his own again. Ah reckon old Joe's murder was probably the work of a couple of free-lances – mebbe Cadman and another man – Ah hardly fancy Fernicutt, Jackman or Carmenito would bother with an old prospector an' his little bag of gold-dust....'

Pete thought of the paper reposing behind the photo in his vest-pocket but he kept his mouth shut.

'Who was the late Mr "Jolly-boy's" partic'ler pard?' asked Hank.

'Wal, that's purty hard to answer. He knocked-around quite a bit. Ah could make out a list of the folks he's bin seen with lately an' make enquiries.' The marshal sighed. 'But yuh don't get much co-operation in this town.

'Wal, ah guess I'd better find my deppity an' give him orders to fetch up ole Joe's body. Then ah suppose ah must go an' break the sad news to Miss Stella. I don't like the job, gentlemen, I don't like it. I'd like to get hold o' the man who killed ole Joe.'

'So would we, marshal,' said Hank. 'We've got a personal score to settle with them bushwhackers.'

'Can Ah see you gentlemen tomorrow mornin' about eleven?'

'Shore you can, marshal.'

'Ah'm trustin' yuh, mind.'

'That's mighty fine of you, marshal,' said Hank as the two made for the door.

'Good-night, marshal.'

'Good-night,' said the big man softly.

Looking over his shoulder before he closed the door Pete saw him standing motionless in the middle of the floor, the shot-gun like a toy in his huge hands.

THREE

Outside, Hank said: 'He takes some weighin'-up, that bozo. Even now I'm not sure whether he believed us or not.'

'Yeh, he certainly is a cunning customer. He has to be to survive here,' said Pete.

'Wal, we'll let him be for tonight anyway,' said Hank. 'I vote we make our way to the "Palace" now. Mebbe we'll meet up with this Sam Fernicutt.'

They walked lightly, fingers brushing gun-butts, eyes alert. They didn't intend to be caught napping.

They swung open the batwings of the San Diablo Palace and were greeted by a blast of cigarette smoke; a blare of noise; the tinkle of a piano, the scraping of a fiddle, the jabbering of innumerable voices. The place was packed now and they had difficulty in worming their way to the bar.

Once there however, they caught the pallid-faced barman's eye and he came over to them.

'We're ready for that supper now,' Hank told him.

'Want it up in your room?' asked the barman. 'I can get it sent up if you do.'

The partners exchanged glances.

'No,' said Hank. 'We'll find ourselves a corner of a table someplace.'

'Suit yourself.' The barman shrugged and departed.

Ten minutes later the pimply vicious-looking youth appeared with the eats on a tray. He led them over to a table in the corner where four dance-girls sat.

'Vamoose,' he snarled.

'Hark at Marty,' giggled one of the girls. 'Tough Marty.'

Marty placed the tray deliberately on the edge of the table and, reaching across, slapped the girl across the mouth with the back of his hand.

Hank gripped the youth's shoulder.

'Take it easy, sonny,' he said. 'The girls 'ull move, won't you, girls?'

'Sure, old-timer,' said the brazen-faced hussy in a particularly low-cut dress. She led the way and the others followed.

The youth turned as Hank let go of his shoulder. His eyes burned but he did not speak. He slouched away.

'Tough Marty,' echoed Pete and he laughed. He stopped abruptly. The youth had looked back. Pete had the uncomfortable feeling that he had heard.

'Hornery little cuss,' he said as he sat down to his meal. He felt vaguely sorry for the youth. He probably had ambitions of a better life than that of being a two-bit lackey in a saloon. Probably he fancied himself a king-pin. Pete wondered what Marty would do if he offered him a tip.

The meal was good. The partners did it justice. They were mopping-up their plates when two percentage-girls came to the table.

'How about a dance, old-timer?' said one who, despite her plucked eyebrows and rouged cheeks, was obviously a middle-aged woman. She put a powdered arm round Hank's neck and leaned her flabby body against his.

Hank's face tightened and he went pale.

'Not tonight, honey,' he said, huskily, trying to appear friendly.

'Aw, c'mon, a li'l dance won't hurt yuh,' said the woman hitching herself on his knee.

Meanwhile, the other one, a younger girl, thin as a willow, had plumped herself on Pete's lap. She slid a thin arm around his neck and caressed his chin with nervous fingers. Almost mechanically, Pete put his arm around her waist, feeling the pitiful bone of her hip through the thin dress. He was watching his pard.

Hank was trying to gently disengage the woman's arm from around his neck. She was half-drunk and she clung to him all the tighter.

'Not tonight, honey,' said Hank. 'I'm tired.' He tried to appear jocular. 'I'm not so young as I used to be.'

Pete pushed his own companion gently away from him.

'I guess it's our bedtime, ma'am,' he said to the woman with Hank. 'Me an' my pard 'uv bin ridin' hard.'

The woman looked up. Her bleary eyes focused on Pete.

'Get up, ma'am,' said he, gently. He took her free arm to help her up.

'Leggo of me,' she yelled. She brought her hand away from Hank's neck and struck Pete across the face. A cheap ring she wore cut a red groove in his neck. She screamed curses.

Hank's control snapped. He snarled like an old wolf as he sent her sprawling from him.

She lighted at the feet of a big, blue-jowled man in a 'prairie-bowler' – a grey bowler hat with a wide brim.

'Yuh shouldn't do that to Sal,' said the big man gruffly. He moved quickly. But he wasn't quick enough.

'Hold it!' a voice barked. Pete, legs apart, had the big man covered. 'I admire your chivalry, muh friend,' he said. 'But I shouldn't follow on if I wuz you.'

The big man let his hands hang lax and eyed Pete sullenly. He did not speak. 'Sal' rose to her feet. She did not make a move to reopen the attack. The nearest people began to press forward.

Hank ranged himself alongside his young companion. His thumbs were hooked into his belt, the right one very near the scarred, walnut butt of his heavy Colt.

'Don't anybody else try anythin',' he said. 'You got anything to settle with my pard, big fella?'

'I guess not,' muttered the man in the bowler.

'Wal, mebbe you'd like to have a crack at me,' Hank continued. 'Guns or fists 'ull suit....'

Another voice answered for the big man. It was sharp, metallic. It said: 'If anybody wants to fight they'd better get outside first.'

The crowd parted and the owner of the voice confronted the partners.

He was tall, straight, well built. He was faultlessly attired in a black, cutaway coat with trousers to match, and shiny, black riding boots with embroidered tops. His spotless white shirt was tied at the neck with a black, 'shoe-string' bow. Crossed cartridge-belts showed where his coat fell open, and revealed also the pearl handles of two heavy guns, well forward for a quick draw.

'Who are you?' said Hank.

The man smiled – a thin-lipped smile beneath the line of moustache in his dark, handsome face.

'My name's Sam Fernicutt,' he said. 'I own this place.'

'And do you allow your women here to pester people?" said Hank smoothly.

Fernicutt smiled again, more affably this time; he almost seemed to wink. 'Not as a rule,' he said. 'If you gents have a complaint to make you'd better come with me to the office.'

The partners exchanged glances.

'Seems like nobody wants to fight,' said Pete with a grin.

'It's underrated, this Diablo,' said Hank drily. He

turned to Fernicutt again: 'Wal, mister, we've no complaint now but we'll still come to your office if you insist.'

'I do,' smiled Fernicutt. 'This way, gentlemen.' He turned.

Obedient to his look, the crowd parted again. Pete and Hank followed him through.

He led them through a trap in the bar, near to the hard-working pianist, and beyond through a stout door marked 'Private'. The office was small, but comfortable and well furnished.

Its main assets were a heavy oak table-desk, a swivel chair, rows of bookshelves along two walls, a tall filing cabinet, and two easy chairs drawn up to a huge empty fire-grate. Fernicutt motioned the two men to these chairs.

'Swing 'em round,' he said. He sat down in the swivel chair behind the desk.

Pete and Hank drew their chairs nearer and faced him.

'Smoke?'

They took an expensive Spanish cheroot apiece from a little carved box on their side of the desk. Fernicutt took an identical cheroot from his top pocket and bit the end off with strong white teeth.

Fernicutt spoke first.

'I guess you're the two the hombres Marshal Withers told me about,' he said.

'You've seen the marshal?'

'Yes. Just before I barged in on your little ruckus. He left me to go and tell Miss Stella, old Joe's daughter, of his death. I don't envy him his job. An' I'm mighty sorry for Stella.'

Pete gave a sympathetic murmur. Hank did not move a muscle. He sat tight-lipped, cold-eyed watching the saloon-owner.

'I'd like to get my hands on old Joe's killer,' said Fernicutt flatly. 'I'd like to know everything you men can tell me about the murder.'

'We can't tell you any more than we told the marshal,' said Pete.

'The marshal's a lazy old skunk,' said Fernicutt, expressionlessly.

'Does that mean to say you think we did the murder?'

The saloon man held up an open palm. 'Hold your hosses, old-timer,' he said. 'I didn't mean to imply anything of the kind. All I meant was I'd like to hear all about the affair from your own lips rather than depend on my friend, the marshal's, hurried, and no doubt garbled, version.'

Briefly Pete recounted their adventures from that morning when they reached the edge of the 'badlands' and hit the Devil's Frying Pan district for the first time. He omitted, however, to refer to the photograph, the torn claim, or the rowel-spike.

'You've been having quite a time, haven't yuh?' said Fernicutt when the young cowboy had finished his tale.

'Yeh, we have,' agreed Hank without a smile. He rose to his feet. 'Wal, now you've heard it all, Mr Fernicutt, we'll leave you to meditate.'

'Have a drink before you go, gents,' said the saloon owner. 'Some of my own special stuff from over the border.' He produced a bottle and glasses from beneath his desk. Hank sat down again. If the man wanted to splash his liquor around the old-timer was the boy to help him. But his face did not relax from its cold immobile mould as Fernicutt poured a couple of generous fingers in each glass. He was weighing-up the suave, gambler-type of gent as if he was some new species of sidewinder who was liable to strike any minute.

Fernicutt raised his glass. 'Here's mud in your eye,' he said.

'Catch it,' said Pete with a grin.

Hank merely grunted and downed his in one.

'Mighty fine stuff this,' said Pete.

The saloon-man looked arch. He almost seemed to wink again. 'You don't get this stuff out front,' he said. As he was talking he refilled the glasses.

The other two were sipping the stuff, really savouring it this time when he said nonchalantly: 'Where you boys from?'

Just as nonchalantly Pete waved a hand. 'All over,' he said. 'We got ants in our pants that keep us on the move.... We've been around,' he added and he meant it in more ways than one.

Hank cut in harshly 'I don't know how you keep so healthy, mister, if you ask all strangers such a lotta questions.'

The two men measured glances. Pete watched Hank's jaw muscles working and he knew the old-timer had taken a violent dislike to the saloon man. The latter's sudden grin did not reach his eyes.

'Don't get me wrong, old-timer,' he said. 'I'm just making conversation.'

Hank downed his drink. He put the glass on the desk. 'All right,' he said. The bottle tilted again. Hank put his hand across the top of his glass. 'No more for me.' Then sardonically: 'If I have too much it might loosen my tongue.' He rose. Pete rose with him.

'I was just trying to be neighbourly,' said Fernicutt unsmiling.

'Sure,' said Pete. 'Thanks.'

As they climbed the stairs to their room the old-timer said: 'There certainly are some cunning customers in this town. I'm no more sure of Mr Sam Fernicutt than I was of his friend the marshal.'

'Nor I,' said Pete. 'These gamblin' sorta gents are plenty hard to figger. They school themselves that way.'

'The marshal admitted Fernicutt was a crook.'

'There's crooks – an' crooks.'

'Yeh – Fernicutt may be a square-shooter.... And he may not!'

By this time they were at the door of their room. Hank, who was in front, opened it. He cursed, his free hand drawing his gun.

Pete, following him, gave an exclamation. The room was in disorder. The beds had been stripped down to the sagging springs. The blankets and mattress – the latter with black flock streaming from them – lay on the floor. The chairs had been overturned. Even the floorboards were ripped up beneath the tattered mats beside the beds.

The uncurtained window was wide-open. Hank ran to it and stuck his head out, his gun ready.

'Purty hopeless,' he said as he turned back to Pete. 'They're probably well away by now.'

'I wonder what they were looking for?'

'Yeh – I wonder?'

The rest of the night passed without incident. The following morning the partners did not tell anybody about the sacking of their room. They did not know who to trust. Least of all yet would they trust the suave owner of the San Diablo Palace. As Hank remarked: he might have engineered the whole thing.

Keeping their promise to Marshal Obadiah Withers they made their way to his office. They met the marshal in the street outside. He greeted them affably; he had been down aways to get some breakfast. A wide grin split and creased his flabby face, his little eyes twinkled in their pockets.

'Ah've got somep'n to show yuh,' he told them as he opened the door of his office. They followed him inside.

'Where's that pesky deppity?' said the fat man. He raised his voice: 'Clem— Hey, Clem!' No answer.

He called again, then led the way through the opposite door, around a corner, along a passage and so through another door which brought them to the cell-block of the jail next door.

'I had this door made specially,' said Withers. 'I usually keep it locked. I don't have much call to use the jail as a rule – most of the badmen here can't be taken alive. But this mornin' ah got me a prisoner ... I guess Clem's in here.' He raised his voice again: 'Clem!' Still no answer.

They passed a row of empty cells. 'Ah want to show you mah prisoner. He's in the end cell.'

He reached it first. They heard him gasp as he looked in. Then he swore a terrible oath. The partners crowded him and looked through the bars of the cell.

Pete, the younger, uttered an exclamation of horror. Hank did not speak. He just expelled a breath through tight lips.

The first thing that met the eyes was the terrible amount of blood in the cell. It was all over the floor and even spattered on the walls and the cot under the window. It seemed incredible that the body in the centre of the floor could have held so much blood.

It lay spreadeagled on its back, a terrible look of agony and surprise on the dissipated, unshaven face, a wide-eyed, accusing stare in the sightless eyes. The throat was cut from ear to ear and looked like a grinning red mouth. Blood was still welling from the torn jugular. The man's arm was in what had once been a white sling, but which was spotted now with red like the rest of his shabby clothes.

Marshal Withers rattled the cell door.

'It's still locked,' he exclaimed. 'Where the hell is Clem? He's got the keys.'

For a moment the flabby peace-officer seemed all to pieces. He seemed more shaken by the disappearance of his deputy than the brutal murder of his prisoner.

He indicated the remains. 'Recognise him?' he said.

Pete spoke. 'I was jest figuring. Yep, I guess so. He's the other one o' the two who throwed-down on us outside here yesterday. I got him in the shoulder, didn't I?'

'That's what I figured,' said Withers. 'Me an' Clem dragged him in on suspicion. He was a special pard o' ''Jolly-boy'' Cadman's. We couldn't get him to talk. I figured if you identified him and he saw we'd got a case he'd spill a line or two.' He sighed and spread his flabby hands. 'Wa-al, I guess somebody made certain sure he wouldn't…. But where's Clem? That's what I want to know.'

Hank McDonald spoke for the first time. He was down on one knee in the passage behind them. 'There's' quite a bit of blood out here,' he said. 'I didn't notice it right away – not until my eyes got accustomed to the light.'

The marshal and the younger man joined him.

'Yeh,' said Pete. 'Look – there's quite a pool by that cupboard.'

'It's the armoury cupboard,' Withers told them, crossing to the tall structure. 'It's full o' spare guns.' He stopped, his hand on the latch. There was a look of almost fear in his little eyes. His face was puckered as if he were about to cry.

'Open it,' said Hank.

Withers clicked the latch and pulled open the door. A sack-like thing fell out against him. He started back with a cry.

'*Clem!*'

The body rolled at his feet.

The deputy's throat had been cut in the same way as the prisoner's. Hank bent over the body. His face was expressionless, only his eyes told his thoughts; they shone with unholy savagery.

'Look at his head,' he said. 'It looks as if he was hit over the head with somethin' first – probably a gun-butt.'

'An the killer cut his throat while he was unconscious – just to make sure,' said Pete. His voice was shaky. He was hard-bitten; Hank and he had seen a lot of sudden death. But he was shocked by the callous savagery of this crime.

Marshal Withers was backed against the passage wall. Two tears coursed down his flabby cheeks. 'We've bin together for nine years,' he said. 'Although I cussed him he was like a son to me.'

The tears were of rage as well as grief. There and then the fat law-officer swore a solemn, terrible oath. The partners stood by in silence. They trusted Marshal Obadiab Withers now. They had seen the real man in that mound of flesh and even in his heart-rending sorrow it was good to see.

'Count us in old-timer,' said Hank softly.

Pete nodded his head wordlessly.

They persuaded the marshal to go back into the office and get a drink of his whisky. His huge body was shaking uncontrollably. The shock of Clem's death and the emotion it had aroused had been too much.

'Go with him, Pete,' said Hank.

When they had gone he bent down and took the ring of keys from the deputy's belt. He went back to the death cell.

Ten minutes later he joined the other two.

'The hombre in the cell was stabbed in the back before his throat was cut,' he told them.

'Who could have done it all?' said the marshal, almost in a whisper.

'He wanted to make certain sure nobody talked,' said Hank. 'I figure he was somebody well known to the prisoner.... He surprised Clem, killed him and took the keys, then went down to the cell and let himself in. The prisoner gets up, probably overjoyed to see him. Somehow the other guy gets around behind him – maybe on pretence o' lookin' through the window to see if everythin' was clear – that wouldn't be hard if the prisoner trusted him – then he stabbed him in the back. He cuts his throat to make doubly sure – I can't figure that really – he'd probably get blood on himself an' all. Anyway, he gets out of the cell lockin' the door behind him.

'I figure he must have killed Clem by this cupboard – there's no blood anywhere else except in the passage. He puts the keys back in Clem's belt and pushes his body inside the cupboard.' Hank turned to Withers. 'Sorry I had to say all this, marshal.'

'That's all right,' said the fat man. 'I'm mahself now. Let's get to work.'

FOUR

'Maybe ah'm prejudiced against greasers,' said Marshal Obadiah Withers. 'But this job seems to have a greaser flavour about it. All that knife-play! We've got desperadoes of our own kind just as callous, but they wouldn't carve two men up thataway – they'd be more likely to favour a gun.'

'Guns make a noise,' Hank reminded him.

'Yeh, that's so. But you can kill a man with the butt o' one. Maybe I'm wrong but I still think this job smells o' greasers. I wonder if Don Miguel Carmenito had a hand in it? He's got hundreds o' knife-slingin', back-stabbin' greasers on his payroll. An' that son of his – that José – he'd be game for anythin' fer all his fancy looks.'

It was the day after the two murders. The three men were seated around the marshal's desk trying to plumb things to the bottom – although they hadn't a single clue.

'What beats me,' burst out young Pete Henderson, 'is that we haven't got a thing to work on. Whoever did the killings – brutal as they were – planned 'em well. He got away clean.'

'There wuz probably more then one,' Hank reminded him.

'Yeh, there's somethin' in that – although it leads us nowhere.'

41

'I did find one thing out,' said Withers. 'I found out that the prisoner's name was Jed Mackey. This morning I let Sam Fernicutt see the body. He knew him right away – said he was an old Texan pardner of ''Jolly-boy'' Cadman – the guy you shot. He joined Cadman here about a month back and they both worked for Fernicutt. But Fernicutt fell out with 'em over some deal or other.'

'What kind of a deal?' said Hank.

'Fernicutt didn't say.'

'Any possibility they might've been workin' with Fernicutt still – when they throwed-down on me an' Pete here?'

'I don't think so. No – somehow, I don't think Fernicutt is mixed up in this. More likely to be the Carmenitos or Ep Jackman.'

'You wouldn't suspect Fernicutt seein' as he's a pal o' yourn,' said Hank.

The marshal was not offended. 'I try to keep an open mind,' he said simply.

At this juncture there came a knock at the outer door.

'C'mon in,' bawled Withers.

They heard the door open and close and the tip-tapping of feet in the short passage. Then the girl stood framed in the office doorway.

Pete Henderson recognised her immediately. He could not mistake the cloud of dark hair, the big, dark eyes, the smile with which she greeted the marshal. 'Miss Stella,' said this worthy, his face creasing as he rose to his feet. 'Come in, my dear. Come in.'

The girl came in and took the seat he put for her.

'Miss Stella Dempsey,' said the fat man, introducing her to the partners. 'These are the gentlemen who – er – found your Dad – Miss Stella.'

'I want to thank you,' she said simply, looking from one to the other. Her voice was low and sad, but admirably controlled.

'We're sorry we didn't get there sooner, ma'am,' said Pete.

Hank nodded in agreement. An almost kindly look seemed to cross his face as he looked at the girl. Even he could but admit there were thoroughbreds in the sex he despised. And here was one of them.

'We're purty certain now that Cadman and his pard, Mackey, were the two who shot your Dad,' Withers told the girl. 'They're both dead now. We want to find the one from whom they took their orders.'

'You think they took their orders from someone else?'

'That's what we think,' repeated the marshal.

'But who would want to kill my Dad?' burst out the girl. 'And why? He did no harm to anyone.'

'I can tell you why, ma'am,' said Pete.

He produced the torn half of the gold-claim from his vest pocket.

'Your Dad had discovered gold,' he said.

'You never told me about this,' said Withers.

'I'm sorry, marshal,' said Pete. 'I meant to tell you yesterday – but so much happened.' He smoothed the crumpled scrap of paper out on the desk. The other three drew their chairs closer. It was Hank, the old-timer, who took up the thread of the discourse with a question: 'Where's the photo, Pete?'

The younger man produced the photo. The girl started as she saw it, but she did not speak.

'The half claim was hidden in the back of the photo,' said Hank. 'We figured the old man had the other half on him, and the killers got that. Now they want this half.'

'But if they get this half of what use is it to them?' said Stella. 'It has Dad's name on it.'

'As long as we have this we have proof of your Dad's claim,' said Hank. 'If they get it they can destroy both halves and jump the claim.'

'If they know where it is.'

'We figured they do,' said Hank. 'Probably the old man had a map or plan an' they got that, too.'

'But wouldn't the agent have old Joe's name on his lists?'

'Yep – together with thousands of others. The agent doesn't know where the claims are. He jest files 'em. An' the trouble is we don't know where the claim is either. If they can get hold of this other half and destroy it – then a mite later they'll suddenly find gold in the Auroras – an' whose to prove it's the old man's claim?'

'But we would find out who did it all,' said the girl.

'Maybe. But I'd figure the king-pin, bein' smart, 'ud have the claim filed in somebody else's name, get somebody else to run things for him – probably a stranger. No, I figure the king-pin 'ud keep in the background. We'd still have nothin' to work on.'

'As far as I can see,' said Pete, 'the best thing we can do is lie doggo – play a waiting game and let the other guys come after this half of claim an' catch 'em at it.'

Withers nodded his head ponderously in agreement. 'The other two murders are tied up with it I figure,' he said. 'If we can find out who done them we'd probably get a lead to who's behind all this.'

'That's what I came about really,' said Miss Stella hesitantly. 'I mean – I wanted to tell you how sorry I am about Clem.'

'Thank you, Miss Stella,' said the fat man. He was strangely moved. 'Don't you worry, Miss Stella,' he continued. 'We'll get who did it. We'll get 'em. We're not lying' down on the job.'

'I know that,' the girl reassured him gently.

'We'll get whoever is behind it all,' reiterated Withers, as if his very repetitious resolutions would bring the man – or men – right into his hands.

The girl rose to go. She shook hands again with the partners and Pete gave her the photo he had found in her father's hut. For the first time since she had entered the room the girl's iron control slackened. Her beautiful eyes filled with tears and clutching the photo in both hands she muttered incoherent words of thanks and, turning, hurried away. Her heels clattered swiftly in the passage and they heard the outer door open and shut behind her.

Turning his head Pete looked through the window and watched her cross the street, a trim, youthful figure in grey skirt with short coat to match, and riding boots. She was bareheaded and the breeze blew strands of her hair from its dark cloud.

On leaving the marshal the partners went back to the San Diablo Palace. The pallid-faced bartender was attending to the customers along the bar, more of them than was usual at this early hour. The one topic of conversation was the murder of Clem, the deputy, and the prisoner, Jed Mackey.

Murders were no rarity in 'The Devil's Frying-Pan' but the calculated brutality of these two had moved even the hardened townsfolk.

As Pete and Hank breasted the bar somebody said to the barman: 'Where's young Marty, Perce?'

Perce's pallid face looked worried. 'I don't know,' he replied. 'He seems to have disappeared. I haven't seen him since yesterday morning.'

At this an excited buzz of talk broke out. Exclamations: 'I wonder if he had anything to do with the murders?' 'Naw, not a kid like him.' 'I dunno – he's a mean little cuss....'

Hank nudged Pete and jerked his head. Pete followed him. They made their way to the corner of the bar which was empty. Hank caught the barman's eye and beckoned him over. Hank placed a cautioning hand on Pete's arm as he ordered the drinks. But when the man returned he said casually: 'What's this about young Marty?'

The man's face puckered. He seemed glad to unburden himself to somebody. He seemed very concerned about the disappearance of his pardner. Maybe the kid had something at that, thought Pete.

'Yesterday morning I sent Marty to the jail with Clem, the deppity's, breakfast,' Perce told them. 'He didn't come back – and I ain't seen him since. I'm afeared somep'n's happened to him. Maybe the murderers kidnapped him or somep'n. No matter what anybody says I still say he couldn't have had anythin' to do with the crime. I know Marty better'n anybody here. He's a good kid fer all his swank. He wouldn't hurt a fly.'

'Hum,' said Hank. 'Has anybody seen him since?'

'The boss's bin makin' enquiries an' he hasn't heard anything…. But somebody jest tole me that Ep Jackman reckins he saw Marty out on the range yesterday.'

'Has Fernicutt seen Jackman?'

'They ain't spoke to each other for years,' said the barman solemnly. 'An' I don't reckon the boss'll break the silence now – even for Marty.'

'Does the boss like Marty?'

'Wal, he allus treats him all right. An' Marty sets the boss up to be a sort of hero.'

'And is he?' said Pete.

'He's allus all right with me,' replied the barman sullenly.

Pete grinned.

'About that breakfast,' said Hank. 'Was Clem, the deputy, used to havin' his breakfast in the jail?'

'Yep, he let me know the night before.'

'An' did he let you know the night before he was murdered?'

'Yep.'

'D'yuh know what happened to the breakfast Marty took over that morning?'

'No.'

'It wasn't anywhere in the jail or office,' said Hank to Pete. 'There wasn't any dirty plates, either.' He turned to the barman again. 'All right – get us another couple, will yuh. An' get one for yourself.'

'Thanks.' The barman took the glasses and went.

When he returned they did not question him further, but tipped up their liquor and with a 'so-long', left the place.

The barman watched them go then turned and knocked at the door of Sam Fernicutt's office.

Hank asked a lounger if he knew where they could find Ep Jackman.

The man pointed to the street.

'S'funny you askin', gents,' he said. 'Jackman went by 'bout ten minutes ago. He went in the Koh-i-nor Eating House. He owns the place, he's got a little office in the back, you'll probably find him there.'

The lounger watched them go reflectively. Then he shrugged his shoulders and proceeded to light the cigar the old-timer had given him.

Ep Jackman was burly, floral-faced. He had little puckered eyes, a wide grin, a booming laugh. His office was in direct contrast to the Koh-i-nor Eating House in which it stood. It was luxurious, the massive oak desk, the padded armchairs, the thick, costly carpet on the floor, all stamped it as the place of a man who loved comfort and yet did not lack in taste.

As Hank and Pete entered his sanctum Jackman rose to his feet from his padded desk-chair and greeted them affably.

'Be seated, gentlemen,' he said.

He gave them cigars and leaning back in his chair with his large, red, muscular hands on the desk in front of him, watched them with a smile as they lit up and got comfortable.

When they were all set he spoke, and his smile faded as he did so – although his voice was still friendly.

'Pellow tells me you want to see me on a matter of grave importance,' he said.

Pellow was the manager of the Koh-i-nor Eating House.

'That's right,' Hank answered him. He introduced Pete and himself.

'I've heard of you,' Jackman told them. 'You're friends of the marshal, aren't you?'

Hank said: 'We're private investigators: Marshal Withers is right behind us.'

'I see.'

'We are now investigating the murder of Clem, the deputy, and that other fellah in the jail yesterday morning.'

'A particularly callous crime by all accounts.' said Jackman. 'But I fail to see in what way I can help you.'

'Wal, I'll tell yuh,' said Hank. 'That same morning, young Marty, who waits over at the Palace....'

'Yeh, I know him.'

'Yesterday mornin' Marty disappeared, an' we've heard since that you claim to have seen him out on the range the same day.'

'I did see him – although I attached no significance to it at the time,' said Jackman. 'You think he had something to do with the murder?'

'We think he might've.'

'And I suppose you want to know where and when I saw him and what he was doing at the time?'

'That's right.'

'I've got a ranch about five miles out of town,' Jackman

told them. 'I usually sleep out there and spend the morning there. Most days I ride into San Diablo after dinner. I did this yesterday, I was about half-way here when I saw Marty. There's an outcrop of rocks a little way off the trail. They're supposed to be the site of an ancient Indian sacrificial temple. Marty was skulking among these.'

'Are you sure it was him? Was he near to you?'

''He didn't come right close,' said Jackman levelly. 'But I couldn't mistake him. He had on that white apron he wears and a short jacket over the top of it. He was on foot. When he saw me he ran like a deer and I lost sight of him among the rocks. I wondered what he was doing out there, of course, but it wasn't important. I rode on. I hadn't heard about the murders, then, of course.'

'That's all you can tell us then?'

'I'm afraid so.'

'Wal, I'm sorry we bothered you,' said Hank. 'Although I think you may have helped us a bit.'

'Surely a kid like Marty couldn't 've done those two murders,' said Jackman.

'I shouldn't think so,' said Hank. 'But yuh never know.'

Jackman saw them to the door and wished them 'good day' affably.

'So that's king-pin number two,' said Pete when they got outside. 'Smarmy sort of a gink, ain't he?'

'I figure that's all a pose,' said Hank. 'He's a cattleman to the bone. Double-faced I reckon him. Yeh – double-faced.'

'S'funny the marshal didn't know about the disappearance of Marty.'

'Wal, neither did we,' Hank reminded him. 'An' we were right on the spot. I didn't miss the little cuss.'

'The marshal saw Fernicutt this morning. He should've told him…. If he did the marshal never mentioned it to us.'

'I guess Fernicutt didn't tell him,' said Hank. 'If he had,

Withers would've told us.'

'Yeh – but why didn't Fernicutt tell him?'

'I guess he thought it wasn't important,' said Hank.

They reached the San Diablo Palace.

'Carry on,' said Pete. 'I want to go some place.'

Hank eyed him quizzically.

'I thought I'd call on Miss Stella,' said Pete almost sullenly.

'All right,' Hank climbed the steps to 'The Palace.'

Pete grinned and set off down the street.

FIVE

He did not hesitate. He knew his direction. He had made sure of the location of Stella Dempsey's drapers shop the day before.

As he walked he unconsciously tidied himself. He readjusted his neckerchief, slapped the dust from his chaps, smoothed the creases from his well-worn Mexican-styled vest. As he ran his hands over the latter he felt something small and hard in the top pocket. He put his hand in and brought it forth. It was the rowel-spike he had found in old Joe Dempsey's hut. How long ago it seemed! The second murders had made him forget the little object and it had worked its way snugly into a corner of the pocket.

He harked his mind back to yesterday morning when they had found the body of Jed Mackey in the cell. No, Mackey had not worn any spurs. Altho' maybe they had been taken from him before he was put there just in case he got any ideas. {Mexican rowels could prove nasty instruments.} If they had been taken from him they might still be at the jail. Pete decided he'd ask the marshal about it and show him the spike.

Stella Dempsey's shop stood a little way back from the main street, and was protected by a low wire fence. From the gate a path led up to the door and the window in which goods were displayed.

As Pete lifted the latch of the gate he still looked preoccupied but, striding up the path, his face cleared, he straightened himself up. The bell clanged above the door as he opened it.

He stood at the little counter, around him shelves stacked with boxes of all shapes and sizes, hangers bearing coats and dresses, rolls of material, hats, yards and yards of ribbon. Then the curtain beyond the counter parted and an Indian girl stood there.

He said: 'Is your mistress here?'

'Missy will be back soon,' said the Indian girl shyly. She vanished. The curtains closed again behind her.

Pete took off his sombrero, put it on the counter, leaned on the counter. He pursed his lips in a soundless whistle. For some reason or other he felt uncomfortable. He waited. The Indian did not return. Pete wondered where her father and the other daughter were. The shop was silent.

Suddenly the bell clanged again as the door was opened. Pete turned, a greeting rising to his lips. He checked it. It was not Stella. It was a young man about the same age as himself, flashily dressed, handsome, dark. A Mexican.

He gave Pete one swift glance from his dark eyes, then ignored him. He rapped on the counter.

The curtain parted, and the Indian girl appeared again.

'Miss Stella?' said the Mexican.

'Missy is not in,' replied the girl.

'That ees is what you always say,' said the man silkily.

'Missy is not in,' repeated the girl stolidly.

The Mexican's white teeth flashed. He was a handsome devil. And very sure of himself. He said:

'Maybe you tell me lies again, eh?' speaking to the girl as if she were a naughty child.

'I not tell lies.'

'You tell lies before.'

'No.' The Indian pointed, shaking her head so violently that the bang of black hair on her forehead waggled and became disarranged.

'Enough of this pretence,' said the man. 'Tell Mees Stella I am here. She will see me.'

The girl continued to shake her head.

'You will not tell her?'

'Missy not here to tell.'

Pete had been watching and listening with a little sardonic quirk at the corner of his lips. He could not hold his tongue any longer. He said, casually: 'She seems on the level.'

The Mexican turned suddenly, black-pencil eye-brows slightly raised, as if he had forgotten all about Pete and was a little annoyed at being reminded of him once more. His quick thin-lipped smile did not reach his eyes. It faded. He was half-turned again, when he said: 'I know these Indians. They are all lies. They do not like me.'

'Can't expect them to if you call them liars.'

The other man chose to ignore this pleasantry.

He said: 'Let me come thru',' and skirted the counter.

'Missy not here,' said the girl. 'You no come in back.' She turned her head and called something in a low voice.

Moccasined feet padded in the back. A tall, gaunt old Indian appeared behind the girl. The girl moved to one side revealing the wicked-looking shotgun in her father's hands.

'You go back other side of counter,' said the old man gruffly. He gestured with the gun.

The Mexican backed away and came around beside Pete. The Indian gestured again. 'Up,' he grunted.

The Mexican brought his hands up above the counter. His eyes blazed. He turned to Pete 'You see that?' he said.

'That low-bred son of a prairie-dog pulled a gun on me.'

'You asked for it, pardner,' said Pete drily.

The Mexican shot him a look of hate, then turned again to the Indian.

'Mees Stella shall punish you for thees,' he said.

The Indian gave no sign of hearing. The gun remained steady as a rock; two sharp black eyes watched the Mexican closely.

Suddenly the bell clanged as the door opened once more, and Stella came in. She took in the situation in one glance.

'Have you been up to your tricks again, José?' she said. 'What's the matter, Poco?"

The Indian replied. 'He tried to come thru' the back, missy.'

'He lies,' burst out the Mexican.

'He tells the truth,' said Pete.

Stella acknowledged him with a smile.

'Who ees thees hombre?' said the Mexican, almost beside himself with rage.

'All right, Poco,' said Stella.

The Indian bowed and lowered the gun. The curtains closed behind him. Then Stella answered the Mexican's question.

'This is Mr Pete Henderson,' she said.

She turned to Pete. 'And this, Mr Henderson, is Senor José Carmenito, who for some obscure reason thinks he has proprietary rights over me. You have just seen an example of his forthrightness.'

'He shore came off second best,' grinned Pete.

José seemed as if he would spring on the cowboy. Then he turned to Stella.

'You would do well not to make fun of me, Miss Stella,' he said silkily.

'Are you threatenin' the lady, hombre?' said Pete.

'Ees that your business?' said the Mexican.

'I'm making it my business.'

The Mexican crouched.

'Hold it,' Pete warned him, thumbs hooked in his belt. He went closer. 'I think you'd better come outside with me an' cool off a leetle. You're in no fit condition to talk to a lady. An' in such a confined space you've kind of gotten in my craw.'

José strode to the door and flung it open.

Pete followed him out.

'I'll call another time, Miss Stella,' he said over his shoulder.

'Please….'

'Don't you worry,' grinned Pete.

He shut the door behind him and turned to meet the onslaught of José Carmenito. An iron-hard fist caught him in the side of the neck and staggered him. Another blow missed him altogether. In his rage José had been too hasty.

As he regained his balance Pete blocked two more blows and by main force pushed José away from the door. He realised he was in for a stiff fight. José was a 'greaser' but he was a thoroughbred. He knew how to use his fists and he was lean and hard.

They clashed again in the centre of the square of soil between the wire fence and the shop. Pete felt a thrill of satisfaction as his fist connected sickeningly with the Mexican's sharp cheekbone. But a right swing from José was already on the way, and Pete stopped it with his eye.

The haze cleared and Pete side-stepped as the Mexican hurled himself from his knees. He regained his balance and turned swiftly. Pete met him with a blow flush in the mouth, another on the side of the jaw as he staggered. But José could take it. He caught Pete's next blow on his fore-arm and retaliated with a blow in the solar-plexus that doubled the cowboy up. Even so Pete managed to dodge the follow-up blow, which whistled past his head. He straightened up, his left arm out like an iron bar, stopping the Mexican dead.

Pete's eye was rapidly closing. José's cheek was a fiery red beneath its tan, his lip was split and the blood trickled down his chin. He evened things up with a blow to Pete's mouth which made the blood spurt. But the cowboy had turned into a merciless fighting machine. Gradually he forced the Mexican back beneath a hail of carefully-placed, agony-inflicting blows.

José had his back against the wire fence. He tried to cover up. Unmercifully Pete punished him about the body. He dropped his hands. Pete let go an uppercut that lifted him over the wire fence and deposited him in the dust of the street.

In his eagerness to make sure his opponent was beaten Pete vaulted over the fence. He landed a little off-balance. As he did so José rose with dramatic suddenness and rushed, his arms pumping.

A blow caught Pete on his shoulder, another on his temple. The last one made the cowboy's head sing. It must have hurt José's knuckles too. But it did not show on his dark face which was a writhing, raging, hating mass. Instinctively, Pete bobbed away, striving to gather his scattered senses.

José came on like a tiger, his white teeth bared. The impetus of his rush carried him right onto Pete. They went down together. José was on top. His right fist rose and fell. Just in time Pete jerked aside his head, which was clearer now. The Mexican hit the ground – hard! He certainly was punishing his hands! But he didn't seem to notice it. His other fist clipped the side of Pete's jaw, making his teeth rattle.

The cowboy shook his head, decided to get out of this

awkward position, and with a mad lunge of his body and hands thrust José away from him. He was on his knees when the Mexican sprang again, his long, prehensile fingers reaching for the gringo's throat. Pete evaded their clutch and caught the other around his hard, muscular body. Locked in each other's arms, straining and panting, they rose to their feet. José's knee punished the cowboy. The latter broke free, pushing the Mexican away from him.

Some of José's rage had left him. Despite his dishevelled appearance and bloody face he looked somehow cooler. Pete watched him warily, shaping like a bantam-cock before the other's arrogance. It was his turn to make the first move: he took two steps, feinted. José was fooled into raising his guard. Pete bent, legs spread, and drove a straight left into the other's middle. José was hard. But not *that* hard. He grunted and doubled-up. A man who feinted with his right in such an unorthodox manner was enough to make anybody wilt. Pete straightened him up again, with his right now, flush under the chin, his knuckles grinding for a moment into the Mexican's throat. José spun away from him. His reactions were those of a born fighter; even as he staggered, having a job to keep his feet, his left arm rubbed across his squirming belly, his right swung over, higher up. He caught Pete's next blow on his right forearm. He began to back-peddle, taking in air slowly, obviously fighting nausea. He covered himself with a scissor-smother that Pete found difficult to break thru'. His blows thudded on rock-hard forearms, on José's shoulders as he swayed, or were deflected onto the top of his head, which wasn't so good for Pete's fists.

The cowboy changed his tactics, crouched low and charged. But José was ready for him now. He raised his fist, brought it over and down. Pete sensed the sweeping rush of it but couldn't get out of the way in time. He was moving though. He received the blow at the base of his neck where it met the padded flesh of his shoulder. With sickening rapidity the ground came up to meet him. He stopped it with his hands, lacerating them in the process. He saw José's heavy boot coming up and scrambled out of the way. He felt the wind of it. Another inch to the left and he'd probably have been a gone goose with half his ear missing. While José was regaining his balance Pete made a rather undignified retreat, backwards on all fours.

The fight although in a quiet part of town had now attracted attention. They had about six spectators, and more were coming.

Pete straightened up. He met José's rush with two rapid blows that stopped him dead in his tracks. One beneath the heart, the other flush in his already battered mouth. He was mad now. Mad with a cold, calculating madness. He didn't seem to feel José's blows any more, but kept boring in, his fists pumping, breaking through the Mexican's guard again and again with sheer brutal strength. He heard the crowd clamouring then, through it all he heard a shrill voice call: 'Stop it! Stop it!' Then again: 'Stop it, I say!'

José was backing away, his head turning. Pete stopped in his tracks and turned, too. Coming down the path from her shop was Stella Dempsey. She had a shotgun in the crook of her hand. Her eyes were bright, her face stern. She was a new Stella to Pete.

She stopped, the gun swung in an arc, its muzzle threatening the little scattering of people outside the gate with the two panting, bloodied contestants in their midst.

'You've done enough fighting for one day,' she said.

The company gawped at her. It was José who broke the spell.

He turned towards his magnificent black stallion which

stood by the gate. He averted his battered, blood-smeared face from the girl as he mounted. She did not speak.

The Mexican turned towards Pete. His dark eyes shone with hate.

'I will remember thees, hombre,' he said. Then he shook the reins and without a backward glance, rode away. Some of the crowd jeered after him. The horse broke into a gallop.

Pete watched him go, his hands hanging laxly, his shoulders stooped. Then as the spectators began to drift away he began to follow.

'Mr Henderson,' said the voice behind him.

'Come inside,' she said. 'And I'll fix you up.'

He hesitated. But, brooking no argument she had turned and was walking back to her open door. He went through the gate and followed her.

As she dabbed his face with stinging lotion she said: 'I was scared one of you might get badly hurt. And all on account of me.'

'That Mex wanted takin' down a peg or two,' said Pete. 'But he shore can scrap. He nearly put paid to me two-three times.'

'He's a dangerous man,' said Stella.

Tact was not Pete's strong point, he said bluntly: 'Why does he hang around? Have you got a soft spot for him?'

The girl was silent for a moment. Her voice was unemotional when she answered. 'José's a friend. I don't like to insult him. He's a bit hard to understand some-times. But I guess you can expect him to be a little touchy. You saw the jeers he got from the crowd. The people of Diablo don't like Mexicans – 'greasers' as they call them. José's father is a big landowner – I dare say his ancestors used to be lords and masters of this territory. José is mighty arrogant.'

'Too arrogant,' said Pete. He felt like arguing with the

girl. After all, he had fought on her account.

She seemed to sense his thoughts. 'I'm grateful to you for sticking up for me,' she said softly. José can be very unpleasant. He might try to…. anyway, look after yourself,' she finished rather lamely.

'I will,' said Pete. He grinned painfully.

'That eye's bad,' said Stella. 'It wants bathing.'

Pete forgot the pain as she bathed the sore spot and stray wisps came loose from the dark cloud of her hair and brushed his face.

He was almost inarticulate when he left her. She brushed aside his stammered thanks. Her shy smile and quiet demeanour hid a real pioneer forthrightness. He turned as he passed through the gate. She smiled and waved to him.

As he got nearer to the San Diablo Palace, the street was busy. Passing folks looked at him curiously.

He entered the saloon and, flipping his hand to the wide-eyed pallid-faced bartender, climbed the stairs to his room. Hank was sitting on the bed cleaning his guns and rifle.

'Gosh,' he exclaimed. 'What happened to you?'

'I just met up with the son of king-pin number three,' replied Pete with a painful grin.

SIX

'No, Ah don't recollect Jed Mackey havin' any spurs on him when we roped him in,' said Marshal Obadiah Withers. 'Or, as you say, we'd've removed 'em. Them Mexican rowels is mighty vicious objects. I don't hold with 'em myself – it ain't right to punish a dumb animal too much…. Still, that's greasers all over – they've got a streak o' cruelty in 'em. I guess it's their nature. You'll have to watch out for that José, young fellah. He's dangerous. An' he's got plenty o' greaser buddies who'd do away with yuh fer a plugged nickel – or less.'

'I'll watch out old-timer,' said Pete. He tossed something in his hand that glittered as it spun in the air. It was the rowel-spike. 'I guess this ain't much of a clue anyway,' he said.

He had a beautiful black eye but, except for that, his face was pretty much the same. The rest of yesterday had passed uneventful, and he had had a chance to put in quite a bit of repair work. Now, the following morning in the marshal's office with the marshal and Hank, he was as spry as ever. His fighting blood was up. He felt like taking on all the greasers in San Diablo one by one. But, as Marshal Withers pointed out, it didn't do to be too cocky;

you couldn't dodge a knife in the back or a shot in the dark. He would have to walk warily.

The marshal spoke again. 'Ah'd like to swear you two hombres in as deputies,' he said.

'That's mighty fine of yuh, marshal,' said Hank. 'Can yuh do it right away – officially I mean?'

'Sure,' said the marshal. 'I can swear in as many deputies as Ah like in a case of emergency. An' I reckon this is one. I'm on mah lonesome now Clem's gone…. You hombres willin'?'

'Sure.'

The marshal reached under his desk and brought forth a huge battered Bible.

That evening. Scene: The San Diablo Palace. It was early yet and the place was not very full. Hank and Pete sat at a table in a corner. They had just finished their tea and, with the 'makings' on the table before them, were rolling cigarettes.

Hank, with his head down, spoke out of the corner of his mouth.

'Those two hombres at the far end of the bar – the big fellah an' the half-breed little cuss – they've bin watchin' us purty closely this last fifteen minutes. Don't look now – I'll tell yuh when to look.'

'Right.'

They bent to the 'makings.'

A few minutes later Hank said: 'Just turn round casually an' glance across the room. They're drinkin' now.'

Pete complied.

'Ever seen 'em before?' said Hank.

'Nope – but they shore look desperate characters. I'd figure they wuz professional gunnies.'

'Wal, we've handled that sort before,' said Hank. 'We'll be ready for 'em if they start anything.'

'Shore thing.'

Presently the 'little half-breed cuss' turned his head and saw the partners looking. He nudged his big companion who turned also. They both looked at the partners. The big man said something to his companion and then strode across the floor. The little 'breed' followed.

'This is it,' said Pete.

'Yeh,' said Hank. 'I've bin waiting for somep'n like this. I'm only surprised it ain't happened sooner. I guess these guys have got our number.'

'I'm surprised they're comin' out in the open,' said Pete.

'I guess they're that confident of their own prowess,' said Hank. 'They're both two-gun men.' He edged his chair a little way away from the table. Pete followed suit.

The big feller halted before them and stood legs apart. His 'breed' pardner ranged alongside him.

'Youse guys seem kinda interested in me an' my pard,' said the big man. His voice was a growl, his attitude menacing.

'We wuz jest sayin' the same thing about you two,' Hank replied levelly. 'I know you've bin watchin' us for the last fifteen minutes, sort of trying to make up your mind to come over. Wal, now you have come, what's on your mind. Who sent yuh?'

'What d'yuh mean, who sent us?' he growled. 'Nobody sent us. We don't know yuh 'ceptin' yuh're a pair o' nosey strangers who seem to be looking for a fight.'

'It's your move,' Hank told him.

While this double-talk was in progress Pete had been watching the little 'breed'. He had seen that system before. One gunny kept the victim or victims occupied with conversation while his pard got the drop on them.

Pete saw the two-gun 'breed's' hand sneak down to his right-hand shooter. Pete half-turned, his own hand sneak-

ing down in a lightning cross-draw. As he pressed the trigger of his Colt he saw from the corner of his eye the big
feller diving for his weapons.

Pete's Colt boomed. The 'breed' screamed. His own
gun crashed as his frenzied trigger-finger contracted. The
slug ploughed its way harmlessly into the floorboards. The
gun followed it with a clatter. The 'breed' clutched his
stomach, pressing it, his face contorted horribly. Blood
came through his fingers. Pete's gun spoke again. The
face dissolved in a mass of blood. The 'breed' went over
backwards. He lay still.

The sounds of Hank's shooting echoed in Pete's ear.
The big feller was on his knees but he still held his gun. It
barked.

Hank threw himself to one side and winced as the slug
nicked his shoulder. He fired across the top of the table.
The big feller's eyes widened, his lips drew back from
yellow teeth in a hideous grimace. The grimace froze
there. The eyes glazed over. The big feller pitched forward
on his face.

'You all right, Hank?' said Pete.

'Yeh – jest nicked muh shoulder, that's all.'

The smoke cleared. Folks came nearer to the table in
the corner. A gradually widening pool of blood haloed the
head of the fallen 'breed' who lay spread-eagled, and was
not a pretty sight. The big feller lay face downwards beside
him as if he had fallen asleep that way.

The partners kept their guns in their hands, casually
covering the crowd. They were taking no chances; the two
gunnies might have friends.

A voice barked: 'Drop 'em!' The office door had
silently opened and Sam Fernicutt stood framed in it, a
sawn-off shotgun in his hands.

Silently Hank and Pete put their guns on the table. No
good ever came of arguing with a man who had the drop

on you with a shotgun. With one pressure of his finger Fernicutt could flatten them both against the wall. The fact that he might hit other people in the process was small comfort. Fernicutt did not seem the sort to let a little item like that deter him.

'Hoist 'em,' said the saloon-owner. 'If there's any more shootin' to be done in my place I'll do it personally.'

The partners raised their hands.

Then another diversion occurred. The batwings swung open and Marshal Obadiah Withers waddled in.

'What's all the shootin'?' he said. Then, seeing Fernicutt, who was right opposite him, 'You look mighty grim standin' there like that, Sam.'

'Better talk to your friends here,' said Fernicutt grimly, jerking his hands in the partners' direction.

Withers turned and looked at them. He eyed the bodies on the floor dispassionately.

'They throwed-down on us, marshal,' said Pete.

'Ye-eh, I guess they did,' agreed the fat man. 'It's their speciality. 'Pears it didn't work this time.' He jerked his head in Fernicutt's direction. 'C'mon in Sam's office.'

'Keep them hands up,' Fernicutt said. 'I'm taking no chances.'

The partners obeyed, Pete grinning.

'Jake, Pete, Joe, Sam,' called Fernicutt. 'Shift the bodies.'

His four minions made their way from the crowd and bent to their grisly task.

Fernicutt, the gun still cocked, ushered the other three men into the office and closed the door behind them with his boot.

Withers turned to him. 'You can put the gun down now, Sam,' he said. 'These two hombres are mah deputies. I swore 'em in this morning. I didn't tell you out there, 'cos I didn't want everybody to know.'

'So,' said Fernicutt. He propped the gun up in a corner. 'How did the ruckus start?' he said.

'Simple,' Hank told him. 'They jest walked across and picked a fight. The "breed" drawed first. They had evidently been sent to kill us.'

'You're bleeding, old-timer,' said Fernicutt.

'Jest a scratch,' Hank told him.

Fernicutt rummaged in his desk and brought forth a roll of bandage and a bundle of cottonwool.

Hank's shirt was torn at the shoulder where the slug had grazed it. Fernicutt tore the cloth and revealed the shallow inch-long crease from which the blood trickled. He swabbed it with the cottonwool, then bandaged it expertly.

'Thanks,' said Hank. 'You ought to 'uv bin a doctor.'

'I was once,' Fernicutt told him soberly.

'Who were those two hombres?' said Pete, jerking his thumb.

'Couple o' professional killers,' Withers told him. 'The big feller was called Big Tom Lowrie, the little "breed" was Piute Joe.'

'Who did they work for?' said Hank.

It was Fernicutt who answered him. 'Nobody. They were freelances. They sold their guns to the highest bidder.'

'Did they ever work for you?' said Hank. He loved sticking his neck out.

But Fernicutt who probably had his measure by now did not seem offended.

'Nope!' he said.

The marshal broke in. 'You figure somebody hired 'em to kill you?'

'Yeh.'

'Who?' said Fernicutt.

Pete answered him: 'That's what we'd like to know.'

Pete lay awake that night trying to pierce the mysterious fuzz that again encompassed his mind. He was groping. The spasm of action that evening had enlivened him – he liked to have something to lay out at. He was not a natural killer, but he felt no compunction about the stamping-out of such bloodstained reptiles as Big Tom Lowrie and Piute Joe. But still he and his pard were no nearer to the solution of the mystery surrounding the deaths of old Joe Dempsey, of Clem the deputy, and Jed Mackey.

Hank McDonald stirred and coughed.

'You awake, younker?' he said.

'Yeh,' Pete told him. 'I'm jest tryin' tuh figure things out.'

'Yeh – same here.'

'About them two hombres we scuttled this evenin',' continued Pete. 'What d'you figure? D'yuh think José Carmenito sent 'em to work off his grudge against me? Or do you think the mysterious hombre behind this claim-jumping racket sent 'em. Tho' maybe Carmenito and the claim-jumpin' gink are one an' the same.'

'Maybe,' said Hank. 'Altho' we *had* figured that the claim jumpin' guy's main object was to get hold of the other half of old Joe Dempsey's paper, which we hold. I guess he'd want to do that in the dark an' in a more subtle way than pickin' a fight in a saloon.'

'Yeh – I guess so.'

They fell silent but, five minutes later, Pete spoke up again.

'I cain't figure about the disappearance of young Marty either,' he said. 'Unless he saw the murderers after they'd done the job, an' they killed him as well to keep his mouth shut. But what did they do with the body?'

'You forget that Ep Jackman claims to have seen Marty out on the range that same morning,' Hank reminded him. 'Your theory makes Jackman out to be a liar.'

'Maybe he is.'

'Wal, why should he say he'd seen Marty if he hadn't?'

'You tell me.'

'I can't – yet,' said Hank. He paused then said: 'Give your brain a rest, younker. Sleep on it. Maybe we'll work somep'n out in the mornin'.'

'All right,' said Pete. He sighed. 'Goodnight.'

'Goodnight,' grunted Hank.

Pete tried to compose himself for sleep, and finally, despite his chaotic thoughts he managed to doze off into a sort of stupor.

He seemed to have been lying like this for ages when some sixth sense warned him that all was not well. He opened his eyes. It was still dark; the moonlight streamed through the open window, and bathed the room in a diffused light. In the glow Pete saw the two men plainly. His hand reached for his gunbelt on the bedrail behind him.

'Hold it,' hissed a voice. 'Another move an' I'll fill yuh full of holes. But if you keep quiet you won't get hurt. Raise your hands. Easy....'

Pete sat up with his hands above his head. Hank rose beside him.

'What goes on?' he said.

'Keep your trap shut,' said the man. He looked tall in the darkness. 'Or nothin' 'ull go on for you any more.'

The moonlight gleamed on the six-gun in the man's hand. Hank did as he was told.

The man's companion, working silently, was going through the partners' clothes. Both their faces were shapeless, masked by dark kerchiefs.

'I've got it,' whispered the second man. He was stocky and broad.

'All right. Open the window.' The other's voice was harsh and grating.

It sounded as if it was studiously disguised.

The second man did so.

'All right. Get out,' said the tall harsh-voiced one.

He climbed through and they heard him drop on the lean-to beneath.

The man with the gun followed him, walking backwards, keeping the partners covered. He put his one leg over the window-sill, then, with a lightning movement, vaulted through. As he disappeared Hank made a swift grab and reached his gun. He dived out of bed and ran to the window.

Hank fired, the shot splitting the night apart, awakening echoes like the roll of drums. Hank was thumbing the hammer; acrid gunsmoke blew back into Pete's face.

Pete clambered into his trousers and boots.

Hank turned. 'They've gone round the corner,' he said. 'Seems like they ain't horsed.' He followed Pete's example. The young man had never seen anybody dress so quickly. Hank didn't wait to get his gunbelt. He went out on to the lean-to, sliding down like a cursing monkey. He held his gun clear.

'Wait for me, you ol' buzzard,' said Pete and followed. People were stirring in the building. Somebody shouted.

Hank disappeared from view. Pete slid down the roof. There was an ominous tearing noise and he felt a draught around his nether regions. He cursed. He was being mighty awkward tonight. When he hit the ground Hank was already running. Pete never ceased to be surprised at his old pard's agility.

He caught him up at the corner. Hank stopped dead. 'Careful,' he said.

Pete almost blundered into him. With one swift movement Hank flattened himself against the wall. Then he stuck his head forward.

'Looks all right,' he said. 'Take it wide.'

He suited the action to his words, backing away from

the wall, making a half circle as he turned the corner. Pete kept pace with him. Then they began to run and the younger man got in front.

He stopped, listening. Panting, Hank caught up. They heard boots-heels thumping in front.

'Come on,' said Pete and darted forward once more.

Behind them at the Palace rose an increasing babble.

Maybe the chasers were being chased too. But they had no time to worry about it. They ran on in the darkness. The stick-up men were being hard-pressed now. Maybe they had not expected to be pursued.

'Keep tuh the side,' yelled Hank.

His intuition was trigger-quick for, even as they swerved, a gun boomed up ahead.

Pete fell to his knees. 'Gosh, that was close! You all right, Hank?'

'Sure.'

They pressed themselves against a rickety fence. Up ahead the thumping feet went on. Behind came the sound of more runners.

'We're bein' followed,' said Pete sardonically, then with another characteristic burst of reckless energy he broke away from the shadows and began to run again.

He saw a single running figure ahead, a dim scurrying shape.

'Hey!' he yelled.

The figure became a motionless blob. 'Hank' yelled Pete and threw himself sidewards as the other's gun boomed, lighting his tallness in the shadows.

Pete retaliated. The tall man began to run again. The odds were against a hit in the dark. Turning his head Pete saw that Hank was still keeping behind him.

'Looks like there's only one of them now,' the younker said. 'They must've split up.'

'Go careful,' said Hank. 'He may be holin'-up somewhere, waiting to drygulch us.'

'Sounds tuh me like they're both holed-up now,' said Pete. 'Tho' yuh cain't hear much cos o' that gol-darned babble behind us.'

'There he goes,' said Hank. They both began to run again. Then the tall figure vanished suddenly.

'He's turned in somewhere,' said Pete. He slowed down a little, hugging cover.

They got to the point where the man had vanished. There was a dark, narrow gully between silent buildings. Up here people were still sleeping the sleep of the just – if not the honest.

All was silent. Behind came the babble. But it came no nearer. The denizens of the Palace and its neighbours were speculative, but not to the point of investigation. Too dangerous! If the absence of Hank and Pete had been noticed it was probable that the people who had been so rudely awakened were inclined to give the 'crazy strangers' more laxity than was usual. If they got shot it was their funeral.

Cautiously Hank and Pete turned the corner into the 'main-drag'. The street was deserted and quiet. The cart-ruts showed like ribbons on the hard, bumpy surface.

Hank snorted disgustedly. 'Seems tuh me both of 'em musta doubled-back. They had all the advantage, pardner, maybe we'd've done better to've got back intuh bed.'

They walked along the boardwalk keeping in the shadows. They reached the front of the Palace. From inside came a subdued murmur. Some of the folks had not returned to bed yet.

'Maybe we better go in the way we came out,' said Pete.

'We can go an' have a looksee round there anyway,' said Hank. 'Maybe we'll pick somp'n up.'

They crept into the alley, worked their way along to the lean-to beneath their open window.

A man stepped out of the shadows. A gun glinted in each of his hands. 'Hold it,' snapped a familiar voice.

He came nearer. 'Fernicutt!' said Pete.

'Oh, it's you boys,' said the saloon-owner. 'What goes on?'

As they told him he holstered his guns. When they had finished all he said was: 'You boys certainly see life….' He paused. Then: 'You'd better go in quietly so's not to cause any more strife.'

As they climbed laboriously up on to the lean-to Pete thought he heard him chuckle.

A little later Hank said: 'Them pesky people certainly worked fast. I never figured they'd try anythin' else tonight. They got the other half-claim, Pete.'

'I don't think they did,' the young man told him.

'Shore they did. That one took it from your pocket. He said he'd got it.'

Pete did not answer. He lit the lamp.

He undid the breast-pocket in his checkered shirt and brought forth the familiar crumpled piece of paper.

'Wal, doggone it!' said Hank. 'Then what was that he took out of your vest-pocket?'

'It was half of my Sharps rifle licence. It was never filled in properly or filed. It was about the same size as ole Joe's claim, an' the same sort of parchment. I jest ripped it in half an' copied the part of ole Joe's signature on the dotted line. In the moonlight I daresay you couldn't tell 'em apart. I reckon it fooled that hombre anyway. I figured it might if they jumped us in the dark.'

'Dadblast me!' exclaimed Hank in admiration. 'An' you reckoned a while back you were not figuring so good. I've certainly got to hand it to yuh, yuh young pup!'

'You allus trained me well, old-timer,' he said.

Hank was thoughtful. Presently he said: 'We'll see what that dadblasted Fernicutt says about all this in the morning. I'm gettin' kind of tired of having him bob up like a jack-in-a-box every time we have trouble.'

'I guess he has tuh look after his own interests,' said Pete.

'Yeh,' said Hank. But he still sounded a little disgruntled. He stubbed his toe and cursed. He mumbled himself to sleep. One phrase that impinged on Pete's consciousness and made him chuckle was 'damned panty-waisted bastard!' It didn't need no guessing about. He knew to whom his cantankerous old pard was referring. Hank's one-track mind was a bit irksome at times…. Still it sometimes paid off.

SEVEN

Adamant and earnest as was the old-timer's resolve to accost the saloon-owner first thing in the morning, Fernicutt managed to reverse the charges by beating him to it. This was due to the lean oldster's regard for his belly. Breakfast was his favourite meal. As Pete was wont to remark 'he didn't now where the ol' buzzard shoved it all.'

Hank was digging into a double-sized helping of bacon, beans and frijoles when Fernicutt appeared in the door of his office. The old-timer was too busy to notice him. But Pete did. Their eyes met.

Fernicutt said; 'Could I see you boys in here for a bit when you've finished breakfast?'

'Sure,' said Pete.

When Hank turned his head the door was closing.

'That's that gent you were so keen on seein' fust thing this mawnin',' Pete told him.

Hank glared and took a swig of coffee. This nonchalant action misfired. The hot liquid went down the wrong way. Hank began to splutter and was hardly helped at all by Pete's heavy hand thumped on his back.

He cursed luridly between spasms of coughing. It was fully five minutes before his face had resumed it's usual

74

leathery finish and he was able to attack his meal once more. But the heart had gone out of him. He left a small portion at the side of his plate.

When Pete pointed this out with mild surprise he was rewarded by a string of loud blood-curdling expletives that made Perce the barman start as if he had received a charge of lead in his backside and turn to stare at the oldster with a look of intense admiration on his usually expressionless doughy face.

The pardners had a smoke and then rose and crossed the room and past Perce to Fernicutt's office. Pete rapped on the panels.

The saloon-man opened the door. 'Come on in, boys,' he said affably. 'Drink?'

'Sure, thanks,' said Pete.

'Not on a full stomach, thanks,' said Hank morosely.

'Take a seat, boys,' said Fernicutt.

He took out the liquor and glasses and poured a couple of fingers each for himself and Pete. Hank watched them with a half-scowl on his leathery visage. Pete grinned at him.

'Now let's hear some more about last night's little ruckus,' said Fernicutt. 'Then we'll get in touch with the marshal. I'm not going to stand for my guests being interfered with in that way.'

'It ain't the first time either,' said Hank.

That shook Fernicutt a little. His eyes glinted. But his voice was level when he said: 'How come?'

'Somebody searched our room the other night while we were down here with you,' said Hank.

'Looks like you've got something somebody wants around here,' said Fernicutt.

'Could be.'

'Maybe if you tell me what it is I can be of more help to you.'

Hank's mouth, opened for a reply, was like a snarl. Pete hastily put his oar in. 'We don't rightly know what it is.'

'So,' said Fernicutt unemotionally.

The silence was pregnant for seconds then he added like a casual afterthought: 'I guess Mr McDonald don't trust me anyway.'

Again Pete's hasty tones answered him: 'It ain't that....'

Hank said: 'Maybe you can be of help to us at that. It seems to me them burglars know their way around here purty-well.'

Fernicutt rose suddenly, his hands on the desk in front of him.

'If you think I've got anything to do with the snoopin' that's gone on in your room you can find yourselves other accommodation.'

'Hank didn't mean that,' said Pete. 'He's jest shootin' his mouth off because he's mad at us lettin' them bozoes get away last night. That's right ain't it Hank?'

'Shore,' grunted the other. The gaze he bent on Fernicutt was free of guile. The saloon-owner sat down. He poured drinks. Evidently it was not his custom to get 'het-up'. But he and the hard-bitten oldster seemed to rub together like two rough flints – until sparks flew!

Hank took the proffered drink this time as if nothing had happened. He downed it in one.

Pete was frowning a little. Usually he was the impulsive firebrand member of the team. Except when Hank had these spells – taking violent dislike to certain people. Then there was no holding him and his native caution was a thing of the past to be used against his gay pard but thrown to the winds as far as he himself was concerned.

Maybe Fernicutt reminded him in some way of that gambler who had done him wrong so many years ago. Did bitter memory live that long and was it strong enough to be rekindled so devastatingly? Hank never spoke of the past, lived always in the present. Was that part of it only Pete's young fancy? Maybe Hank had a hunch. Maybe he had got something here after all. Looking at the poker-faced saloon-owner Pete could not think. He did not dislike the man as Hank did. He almost liked him. But wasn't being charming to people part of his stock-in-trade! Pete was getting hog-tied with his thinking.

The subject of his speculations smiled and spoke.

'Well, gentlemen, what do you say we pay a call to our old friend, Obadiah Withers? Something may have turned up that will throw light on the mysterious happenings around here.'

They found the marshal in his office. His feet came off the desk and he reached for his gun as they entered. He looked startled. He shrugged his huge shoulders and relaxed again when he saw who it was.

'Cain't a man never get no peace?' he said. 'What's bitin' you three?' He put his feet up on the desk once more.

The three men sat down around the room. Fernicutt did the talking.

When he had finished Withers said: 'Yuh know – Ah thought Ah heard some shots last night. I thought maybe it was a drunken cowboy out late. The ruckus didn't last long. I figured it was no good spoilin' my beauty sleep jest fer a drunken cowboy.'

'It was no drunken cowboy,' said Hank harshly. The people in this town were beginning to get his goat.

'You take the biscuit, Obey,' said Fernicutt. It was the first time the pardners had heard the huge man called by his first name in that way. It sounded kind of silly some-how.

'Nobody got a good look at the burglars then?' said Withers.

Pete said, 'Like I told yuh they was masked. All I know

is that the one who carried the gun and did the talkin' was a tall hombre with a harsh voice – I guess his voice was disguised tho'. It didn't sound natural tuh me.'

'It was disguised all right,' said Hank. 'The other man was kinda short and broad – kind of hunch-shouldered.'

'That helps us a 'ull lot,' snorted Obadiah. 'Might be almost anybody in town. About coupla dozen guys in town answer to both them descriptions.' His feet thumped on the boards. He rose with a heavy grunt. The chair gave a squeak of relief as he left it.

'Wal, I guess we shan't get no place sittin' around here.'

'Well, I got to get back to my place,' said Fernicutt. 'Let me know if anything turns up.'

He made for the door. As his hand reached for the latch the door crashed open. A man came through, bumped into him. Fernicutt cursed, pushing the man away from him. The latter was oldish, tow-haired, vacant-faced. He looked kind of scared.

'Marshal Withers,' he babbled. 'I found a daid body – a daid man back of my place – throat cut – horrible! – in the old lean-to back o' my place.'

'Take it easy, George,' said the marshal. 'Come on. Show us.'

George Mulbern kept a small dirty general-store a few doors away from the Palace. He was a misfit in Diablo, a timid dim-wit who came from no one knew where; most of his customers blatantly robbed him. He scuttled in front of the four men, babbling incoherently, darting little quick glances all around him, scared but kind of proud of being somebody for a change. A dead body in *his* outhouse!

People were coming in all directions and congregating around his place as the four men got there. George had evidently blabbed quite a bit before he got to the marshal's office.

Fernicutt had forgotten about his business at the Palace. George led him and the three other men around the back of his dingy stores. There was already a bunch of people around the door of the sagging outhouse.

'Break it up,' said the marshal roughly.

He went through them under a head of steam. The others followed. The four of them crowded into the small lean-to. It was disused, its floor of sod strewn with old rusty waggon-parts and other miscellaneous rubbish.

But all eyes were impelled to the thing there in the corner sitting right in the beam of morning light that came through the cracked dusty window. At first sight it looked like a bulky grinning doll. But they did not need to investigate to know it was really the remains of a man.

The head was thrown sideways and back, almost severed from the body. A gaping red gap grinned at the onlookers. The man's shoulders and shirt front were dyed crimson with dried blood. He sat in a pool of it. The stench was sickly-sweet, killing all the other odours of George's filthy little outhouse. The dead man, now a shapeless bundle of leering death, had been a broad stocky muscular specimen.

'It's "Grip" Scanlon,' said Fernicutt.

'Shore 'nough,' said the marshal. 'No loss to the community I guess.' Despite his seeming callousness, the fat man looked kind of sick.

'Another hardcase?' said Pete.

'Who'd he work for?' said Hank.

'Nobody in particular,' said Fernicutt. 'He'd got plenty more brawn than brains. He'd do anythin' for anybody for a few dollars.'

'Mackey, Clem, an' now ''Grip'' Scanlon,' said the marshal half to himself. '*God.*'

Hank stepped gingerly nearer to the body. He bent and picked something up from the edge of the pool of blood.

It was a navy-blue bandana, spattered here and there with small spots of dried blood. He held it up.

Pete's quick mind worked the same way as his pard's. He spoke his thoughts: 'Looks like he wuz one o' the bozoes who came intuh our room last night. The broad, stocky fellah.'

'Yeh,' said Hank. 'It's him all right.'

'No wonder we lost him,' said Pete. 'He must've bin lying here all the time. Only one thing could've happened to him – that tall hombre suttinly has a rough way with his pards.'

'Payment in full,' said Hank. 'An' no come-backs.'

'He must be a maniac,' burst out Pete. 'Shorely there wasn't no need fer that. The dirty, sidewinding murderous snake!'

'Yeh, he's got his own methods too. Messy but mighty effective.' Hank made another stride forward, caught hold of a blood-stained shoulder and jerked. A horrible shape-less bundle, the body rolled forward.

Wiping his hands on his chaps, a grimace of distaste on his lined face, Hank said: 'Look at his back.'

Both Pete and Sam Fernicutt, hard-bitten though they were, could not suppress a shudder. The man had been stabbed three times in the back.

'A strong man did that,' said the saloon-owner. 'The poor devil was dead before his throat was cut. Seems like the work of a lunatic.'

The marshal, whose guts weren't as stout as his heart, was retching. He recovered himself and turning on the gaping white-faced crowd outside bawled furiously: 'Clear the way there!'

EIGHT

The following morning was the day of the funeral of old Joe Dempsey. A party of his friends, led by Marshal Withers, had fetched the body from the cabin up in the Auroras the day after the murder. Since then it had been lying in state in 'Calico' Parson's Funeral Parlour.

Marshal Withers had elected to have the funerals of Clem and Mackey later the same day. There were no mourners for the latter. His one pard, 'Jolly-boy' Cadman, had gone before him, and had been buried in an unadorned hole in the ground on the fringe of Boot Hill. At least Mackey would have a plain board above his head with his name on it and the date of his death. And who among the vice-ridden denizens of the 'Devil's Frying-Pan', could say he should not be treated thus.

Stella Dempsey, Obadiah Withers, Hank McDonald and Pete Henderson went to the cemetery together.

Stella was admirably controlled. Even when the first spadefuls of clay were falling on the coffin-lid she remained the same; full red lips set and firm, dark eyes looking straight ahead into distances where no one else could follow.

The funeral was a real old Western one. Everyone

81

walked at a very slow pace, the bearers, four old-timers who had known and loved old Joe, carrying the coffin on their shoulders. Even the folks who brought horses along walked them. There was no conversation and every man carried his hat in his hand.

The journey back was the same. Not until all were back in the San Diablo Palace would the eating and drinking, the custom with funerals the world over, begin.

Stella Dempsey wanted no part of this. She walked well in front with her escort: Hank, Pete and the marshal. So it was they who were the first to see the horseman with his burden coming down the street towards them.

He was a stranger in town; a pudgy, pale-faced individual in a black frock-coat and black Stetson. Pin-striped trousers were tucked into plain black riding-boots. He rode his brown gelding awkwardly. Over the saddle in front of him was slung something that at first sight looked like a sack, half-full, slack, dangling each side of the cantle.

'Take Miss Stella on ahead, Pete,' said Hank.

Hank watched them go and then in four long strides was beside the horse as they halted in the middle of the street. He lifted the burden gently from the saddle and held it cradled in his arms. Puffing, Marshal Withers was beside him. They looked down into the white, dead face of young Marty. His mouth was open, his eyes staring like a frightened child's. He still wore the apron in which he had worked at the Palace, but now it was no longer white. The breast of it was stiff and brown with dried blood, torn where the bullets had entered through it and into the frail body beneath.

Marshal Withers groaned. Hank cursed softly, savagely. He was the first to recover. 'Quick! Into the office before the mob gets here.' He turned to the silent rider. 'You too, stranger.'

The stranger dismounted and followed them in.

Hank placed the body on the small couch against the

wall and sat at its feet. The marshal, breathing heavily, leaned against the wall by the window. The stranger sat down in a chair.

'I found him just off the trail about two miles out of town,' he told them. 'He'd been there a bit. The buzzards were beginning to settle an' come near. It was them that made me notice. I was only just in time to save him from them. They hadn't touched him.'

The stranger had a flat tuneless voice. No traces of emotion showed on his clean-shaven, pudgy white face.

'He'd been missin' a coupla days,' put in Withers huskily.

'Perhaps I'd better introduce myself,' continued the stranger. 'My name is Jonathan Helliwell. I sell patent medicines. My waggon, with my two assistants, will be along presently.'

'They don't go for that kind of thing here,' said Withers dully. 'This is a tough town.'

'So's Tombstone,' said the stranger. 'But I sold plenty there. I don't scare easy, Mister Marshal.' His voice remained tuneless, matter-of-fact.

'You don't carry a gun,' said Withers.

Helliwell reached downwards swiftly and produced a small but wicked-looking Derringer from a cunning hiding-place in his boot.

'I don't like usin' this,' he said. 'But I can if need be…. An', I might add, both my assistants carry guns – and they're fast.'

'We've got 'em faster here' said the marshal.

Hank felt irritated with the fat lawman. He seemed bent on carrying on a childish argument with Helliwell. He broke in with: 'Can't you tell us anythin' else about young Marty here, Mister Helliwell?'

'I guess not,' replied the man. 'I'm sorry. I should like to have gotten a shot at the skunks who did that to him.'

He turned suddenly back to Withers: 'I might add, Mister Marshal, I have an old Sharps on my saddle-horn an' I'm a dead-shot with it.'

Helliwell turned to Hank again and continued:

'There was nobody in sight. I hadn't seen anybody in fact since I left Don Miguel Carmenito's hacienda up against the border.'

'You know Don Miguel?' said Withers.

'I didn't. I do now. We just stopped there to water the horse an' pass the time o' day. The Don himself called us in and gave us a meal. An hospitable old cuss – an' a real gentleman. He complained he had a cough so I gave him a bottle of my special cough-cure as a present. He wanted us to stay the night. Proper old Spanish grandee…. I left the boys hitchin' the horses an' came on ahead. I reckon they'll be here pretty soon now.'

Withers went off at a tangent. He did not seem to have been listening to Helliwell. He said:

'Maybe we'd better go take a look at the place where you found the body.'

'Well, I don't think you'll find any clews, marshal,' said Helliwell. 'But I'm willin' to go along with you an' show you the place. I want to met my boys, anyway.'

'We'll go into Calico's Funeral Parlour first an' tell him he's got another customer,' said Withers. A tremor in his voice belied the callousness of the words. He led the way out, a ponderous and rather hollow personification of justice – lumbering like a young buffalo.

Calico Parsons was not to be found in his funeral parlour.

'I guess he's in the Palace with the rest of 'em,' said Withers.

Sure enough he was. He was a stocky, red-faced man with a paunch. The black habiliment of his profession was enlivened by a bright red kerchief knotted at his throat and clasped by a tiny gold horseshoe pin. He had a little nervous laugh.

He greeted them heartily and invited them to have a drink, but when he heard the news his face sobered.

The four men formed a little knot at the bar. They pitched their voices low. Others in the saloon looked curiously at the stranger, Helliwell with his pale, pudgy face and his black frock-coat. He was no ordinary cowhand or saddle-tramp, yet he didn't look like a gambler or a gunman. He was kind of hard to place.

'Where's the body?' said Calico professionally.

'In my office,' Withers told him. 'We'll take you there now.'

The man supplanted the undertaker and Calico said with genuine feeling: 'Pore young Marty. He wasn't a bad kid underneath y'know.'

Perce, the barman, had just stopped at his elbow with another drink.

'What's that about young Marty?' he asked sharply.

Quietly, the marshal told him.

Perce's flabby white cheeks quivered, his eyes blinked. 'Pore Marty,' he said softly. Then louder, almost savagely. 'He *was* a good kid. He *was*....'

'We know that Perce,' said Withers. 'But have you any idea who could have done this to him?'

Perce's face became set. He said, soberly, 'I wished I had. He musta seen the men who killed Clem and that Mackey, an' they seen him. I guess he got scared an' ran away. Marty wasn't brave altho' he pretended to be tough. He was just a kid. I guess they caught up with him. He ought to 'uv come to me. He ought to 'uv....' His voice rose, he thrust his white face forward at Withers. 'What are yuh goin' to do about it, marshal?'

'Everythin' we can, Perce,' Withers told him. 'We're goin' to the place now where he was murdered.'

The four men went out. Perce stared after them until they disappeared, and then he turned and knocked at the door of Sam Fernicutt's office.

Ten minutes later Hank McDonald, Marshal Obadiah Withers and the medicine-man, Jonathan Helliwell, rode out of town.

Halliwell led the way. About two miles out he veered off the trail.

'The body was just beyond that patch of cacti,' he said, pointing.

As they reached the spot two buzzards rose from the ground and wheeled away with shrill cries.

'He'd lost blood,' said Helliwell, soberly. 'That's what they're after.'

'Pesky critturs,' growled Withers. 'Look around for footprints or hoof-prints.'

They did not find any footprints. If there had been any in the sand surrounding the body the buzzards had obliterated them. But, a few yards away, in another soft spot close to the cacti patch, they came upon hoof-prints.

Withers went down on one knee and examined them.

'These can't help us much,' he said. 'They're just ordinary; could've bin shod anywhere. One of 'em's got a split at the side here, that's all.'

'It's worth remembering anyway,' said Hank.

Helliwell gave an exclamation and bending, picked up something that glittered. The other two went to him, peered at the silver disc that lay in the palm of his hand.

'Hell! Just a cent,' said Withers disgustedly.

They covered the ground thoroughly for yards around, but did not find anything else. Finally they gave it up and rode back on to the main trail. It was then they saw the dust cloud.

'I'll wager that's my boys with the waggon,' said Helliwell.

Hank nor Withers did not seem inclined to wager with him. They would have lost if they had, for the dust cloud did indeed dissolve into a covered waggon drawn by two horses.

It was the 'prairie-schooner' type, the canvas was white and the chassis was painted a brilliant mixture of yellow and crimson. The horses were both chestnuts; they glistened with health and good grooming and each had a scarlet plume nodding on its forehead.

On the driver's seat side by side sat a big man and a little man. They waved their hands and chorused: 'Howdy, boss!'

'Howdy, boys,' Helliwell replied as the waggon drew up alongside. He introduced the boys to Hank and the marshal.

The big man was called Jack. He was cheery, moon-faced; strands of yellow hair stuck out like straw from under his battered Stetson. He looked like a Swede but he did not speak like one.

'Any friends of the boss's are friends o' mine,' he said.

The little man said: 'Hear, hear.'

His handle, for some obscure reason, was 'Bicker'. He was wizened and yellow like an old man, but, for all that, he seemed to irradiate energy. He grinned, showing small buck teeth like a rabbit's. His little eyes snapped like sparks.

The riders fell in beside the waggon and they set off again.

'The old Don sent you on your way with much rejoicing no doubt,' said Helliwell.

'Wal, no, he didn't,' big Jack told him. 'Yuh see a gang o' punchers rode in jest as we finished gettin' the hosses ready. They were led by a tall handsome-looking young Mex. Wal, handsome I say – his face looked as if it had bin thru' a mincin' machine....'

Hank permitted himself a thin-lipped smile as he said: 'Yeh, we know, that 'ud be José, the old Don's son; my young pard, Pete, worked him over the other day.'

'He suttinly made a good job of it,' grinned Jack. 'We figured it was the old guy's son by the hullabaloo his arrival created an' by the way he ordered everybody about – a wicked-lookin' young hombre. He was in a hell of a temper. The old man was all of a dither when he saw him. I guess he didn't see us slip away.'

'I shouldn't like to work on that spread wi' that young hellion ramrodding it,' put in little Bicker.

They rode into the main street of San Diablo and caused a mild stir among the loungers therein. But altogether it was a triumphal entrance. The marshal's presence carried weight in more ways than one; and if Helliwell had any trade at all, a lot of it would no doubt be due to that fact. The death of Marty was fresh too, and maybe Helliwell would gain a little notoriety as the man who found the body. Still, bodies were ten a penny in Diablo and patent medicines were something new. A new diversion.

As the waggon passed the undertaking parlour Calico Parsons ran out.

'Marshal,' he called.

Helliwell jerked on the reins. The vehicle rumbled to a stop. The marshal and Hank climbed down.

'Come on in here,' said Calico.

The front part was just a bare cubby hole with a dusty counter. There was a fat dusty register in which Calico was supposed to note down deaths and births, if any but seldom did. The paunchy undertaker lifted a trap aside and opened another door. He led them through into his inner sanctum. It was a medium-sized barn-like place. The very chill air of it was permeated with the smell of death. That never seemed to bother Calico, timid though he was. But the other two recoiled a little from it. Calico slept in a bed-sitting room at the side of this place. The dead held no terrors for him – it was the too-boisterous living he feared.

The death-parlour was bare, swept and garnished cleanly. Calico laid his customers out on plank-trestles, of which there were seven. Two of them now were occupied by blanketed forms, those of Grip Scanlon, all stitched up nice and tidy, and young Marty. Calico crossed to the latter and drew back the rough, horse-blanket. He had closed the fear-ridden eyes and the contorted mouth, and the kid's face looked more peaceful.

Silently the three men looked down at him. The marshal and Hank waited for Calico to speak. Finally the undertaker said: 'Marty must've got right close to the man who killed him – must've tried to fight him off even. He must've been gamer than we thought.... I got somethin' tuh show you.'

He led them through another door into his own dusty quarters. The subtle odour of death even reached to here. It looked like Calico kept his windows closed all the time. Behind his back Marshal Withers wrinkled his nose with distaste.

Calico crossed to a cupboard beside his unmade bed with its dirty sheets and ragged counterpane. He opened the cupboard door and delved inside, grunting a little.

'This was clutched tightly in Marty's hand. It's a piece o' stuff from somebody's shirt.'

The marshal took it from him. He and Hank scrutinised it closely.

'Some shirt!' said Hank. 'The hombre who wears that must be a real dandy.'

'A dandy killer!' said Withers.

The material was a brilliant green with red stripes – or maybe it was checked – the piece was not large enough to allow them to make sure.

'Shorely there's no two men in this territory wearin' a shirt like that,' said Hank. 'When we find a man wearing one like it we'll maybe be nearer tuh findin' out who killed Marty.'

'An' Clem,' added Withers. He looked up at the undertaker. 'I'll keep this.'

'Sure, Marshal,' said Calico. 'Anythin' I can do….' He did not finish the sentence but spread his hands in an eloquent gesture. For a moment his weak little eyes were no longer timid.

As the marshal, Hank and Pete left the undertaker's they met Stella Dempsey. She had heard what had happened. Pete said he would walk along with her and explain. They left Hank and the marshal and walked on.

'Who was it?' said Stella, looking straight in front of her.

'It looked like young Marty,' Pete said. 'He's been missin' a coupla days.

'He was dead?'

'Yeh, I'm afraid it looked that way.'

'Killings – killings,' said the girl softly, bitterly. 'Who can be at the bottom of them all? He must be a fiend.'

'We're doing our best to find out who is at the bottom of it all,' said Pete 'We figured Marty might tell us somethin' if we found him. I guess they got to him first. Either he was mixed up in the murders himself, or he saw the men who murdered Clem an' the other guy that morning.'

'I suppose that was what happened,' said Stella. 'He was only a boy. I reckon he got frightened.'

'Yeh….' Pete went off at a tangent. 'Can't you give us a clue at all, Miss Stella? Don't you know anybody who might've wanted to harm your father? Maybe for another reason apart from getting his gold?'

'Father was well-liked,' said the girl softly. 'If only I could help…. But I can't. They were after his claim, thats evident. Why, this town is full of thieves and murderers who would kill their own mother for much less than that.'

'You're goin' to stay here, Miss Stella?'

'Yes,' said the girl. 'I want to see this thru' to the end. Don't you worry, my Indians will look after me.'

A compliment rose to Pete's lips and was checked by a deep voice saying: 'Good morning.'

It was Ep Jackman. He paused, taking his hat off to the girl.

'I'm sorry I couldn't get back in time for the funeral, Miss Stella,' he said. 'I should've liked to have been there – I was proud to call your father my friend – but I had to go over the border on business. It was unavoidable, I'm afraid.'

'That's all right, Mr Jackman,' said the girl. 'I got your wreath. It's lovely.'

Jackman smiled. 'I'm glad you liked it.'

He turned to Pete. 'I want to congratulate you on your magnificent handling of our young Mexican friend the other day,' he said. 'It was time he had a lesson.'

'Always happy to oblige,' grinned Pete.

'Any champion of Miss Stella's is a friend of mine,' said Jackman effusively. He bowed and passed on.

Stella and Pete walked on. 'He was a friend of my father's,' said Stella almost to herself. 'But I've never liked him. Maybe that's just because he's too fussy…. I don't know…. He's a big man here and they do say he hasn't got to the top by fair means.'

'He certainly knows what goes on in this town,' said Pete reflectively.

NINE

The habitués and regular customers of the San Diablo Palace had gotten used to the two men at the corner table: the lean, grim old-timer and his young panther-like companion. Speculations about them were rife, but, since the sudden deaths of Long Tom and Piute Joe, not outspoken.

It was the general impression that they were some kind of lawmen here to give the marshal a hand. They always sat at the same corner table to eat, smoke, talk and watch. They interfered with nobody and the lawless rank and file of Diablo did not interfere with them.

Some, who pretended to be in the know, said there were powerful elements pitted against them, and they were riding for a fall. Meanwhile the two men sat at their table, slept in their room upstairs, or roamed around the town and the surrounding ranges carrying on silent, obscure investigations of their own.

The day after old Joe Dempsey's funeral and the discovery of Marty's body, at about 9.15 in the evening, Pete and Hank sat at their table, with the 'makings' before them, rolling smokes and talking.

The night life at Diablo was just about getting under

way, and as usual The Palace being the biggest and most popular honky-tonk in town, was packed to the doors and windows. The air was thick with smoke, and laden with the aroma of unwashed bodies and whiskey. Now and then as one of the girls passed the corner table the partners got a whiff of cheap scent. None of the girls deigned to pause there, however. They feared a repetition of the incident that happened a previous night when Hank McDonald demonstrated pretty forcibly his opinion of the fairer sex and especially of percentage girls.

The fat pianist, helped out tonight by a fiddler and a concertina player, was rattling out dance music for the uncertain benefit of couples who shuffled on the square of sawdusted floor that was cleared for the purpose.

Customers at the bar were lined up two deep. Perce, the pallid-faced barman cursed monotonously as he served and sweated, but he did not change colour. Another older man was assisting him in place of the deceased Marty, who by now was probably forgotten by most of the people who clamoured at the bar and who had doubtless been served countless times by the dead youth.

Marty's body lay next-door-but-one in Calico Parson's Funeral Parlour awaiting the ministrations of that jolly individual who at that very moment, oblivious of his charge, was leaning over the bar being served by the dead younker's successor.

But at least two individuals in that screaming, shouting, dancing, singing mass of vice and iniquity remembered Marty and deigned to speak of him.

'D'yuh think maybe the kid was mixed up in the murders – maybe even had a hand in 'em – an' fell out with his pard or pards?' said Pete Henderson. 'Or maybe he was jest killed to keep his mouth shut after he'd outlived his usefulness.'

'Maybe,' said Hank McDonald. 'I can't figure…. Maybe

the killers used the kid for a decoy to put the deputy off
his guard…. Altho' everybody seems to be givin' him a
good name now he's dead.'

'Some folks gave Billy the Kid a good name after he was
dead,' said Pete laconically. 'I guess private investigators –
an' that's what we crack ourselves up tuh be lately – hadn't
oughta listen to sentimental gossip led, very cleverly, I
guess, by the dead kid's pardner – one Perce.'

Hank shook his head almost sadly: 'I've seen many a
bad man weepin' in his cups,' he said. 'Personally, I cain't
say I like that Perce, but his sorrow may be genuine. An'
Marty may 'uv been a good kid.'

But Pete was not listening. He had turned round
towards the door. 'What's goin' on?' he said.

There was a commotion around the batwings. A phrase
was passed along from mouth to mouth.

'*Ep Jackman's bin shot.*'

Jackman was a mighty important person in town and
this phrase naturally caused quite a furore.

'C'mon,' said Hank rising to his feet, all thoughts of
Marty fled from his mind.

Pete followed him, hoping maybe there'd be a call for
some action. They pushed their way to the door, breasted
the batwings and were soon outside. But many others had
gotten the same idea and, being nearer the door than the
partners, had gotten quite a start. The street was full of
people. They were streaming towards the Koh-i-nor Eating
House.

They got inside the eating house where Pellow, the little
manager, was stamping about and wringing his hands
while a group of men tried to break down the door of
Jackman's office, and only bruised themselves in the
process.

'Shoot the lock off,' said Hank. He drew his gun. Men
recognised the grim old lawman and his young pard and

stood to one side to let them through. Hank fired downwards, smashing the lock. He and Pete then put their shoulders to the door. It flew open.

'Get a doctor,' yelled Hank.

Ep Jackman was lolling in his padded chair, his head thrown back. His face covered with blood.

'Here's the doc,' somebody shouted.

A little man with a red nose and a hesitating manner was thrust forward.

'I'm Dr Sloane,' he bleated as he joined Hank and Pete by the figure in the chair.

Hank held Jackman's wrist. 'He ain't dead,' he said.

'Keep back,' bawled a voice, and Marshal Withers joined them. Obedient to his command the people came no further than the office door but became jammed there staring and commenting.

The little doctor, who was much more capable than he looked, had soaked a clean white handkerchief at Jackman's water carafe, and was now gently wiping blood from the big man's face.

'He'll be all right,' he said. 'He's just creased along the side of his head. It was a near one tho' – another inch inwards and he'd 'uv been a goner.'

Withers glanced at the window which was open behind Jackman.

'Evidently it was a snapshot from there,' he said. 'An' the would-be killer didn't stay to make sure.'

'Who'd want to shoot Jackman?' said Pete.

'Nobody I could put a finger on straightaway,' said Withers. 'But I guess he'd got plenty enemies – important men always have.'

'He's comin' round,' said the doctor. He fished a flask from out of his hip-pocket. 'Here, Ep, take a drop of this.' He put it to the man's lips.

Jackman took a drop, coughed feebly; the liquor trick-

led down his chin. He opened his eyes wide, shook his
head from side to side. His eyes were still glazed. Then his
full faculties returned. He said:

'Who was it?'

'That's what we'd like to know,' Withers told him.

'Don't fret, Ep,' said the little doctor. Then, turning to
the others: 'Let's get him over on the couch so I can fix
that wound.'

The Koh-i-nor Eating House had been cleared of all
customers and sightseers, and the doors bolted. The
doctor had gone, and Ep Jackman, his head swathed in
bandages, was sleeping on the couch in his office. Over a
table in the eating place the marshal with Hank and Pete
was interrogating Pellow, the little manager. So that they
would not get too dry in the process all were imbibing
some excellent coffee the manager had made.

'There were about half-a-dozen people in the place,'
said Pellow. 'The cook was in the kitchen and Dave and
Mike were serving. I was giving a customer some change
when I heard the shot.'

'Only one?'

'Yes. I ran to the boss's door and tried to open it. It was
locked. By this time Dave, Mike and Carlo, the cook, had
come to help. But I guess we only got in each other's way.
People were coming in from the street and then this gent
indicating Hank came in and shot the lock off.'

'Yuh've got no idea at all who might've taken a shot at
your boss?'

'No,' Pellow licked dry lips. 'Unless it was one of
Fernicutt's gunnies. They've been deadly enemies for
years....'

'Mere professional rivalry I always figured it,' interrupted Withers. 'Have you any grounds at all for your
suspicions?'

'No-o … I guess not.'

The marshal grunted. 'Ah guess none o' your buddies can help us either – hey?'

'I guess not. But I'll call them.' Pellow did so.

Dave and Mike were nondescript youths not unlike the dead Marty had been, but they lacked Marty's singularly vicious expression. They had heard the shot, of course, but otherwise they didn't know a thing.

Carlo was a fat, greasy, middle-aged Mexican.

'Did you hear the shot?' he said.

The Mexican shrugged expansively. 'Sure. Everybody heard eet.'

'An' where were you when you heard it?'

'I was een my kitchen.'

'Anybody with you?'

'No.'

'Has your kitchen got a back door?'

'Yes.'

'Let's take a looksee at this kitchen,' said Withers, lumbering to his feet.

The kitchen was a small, square place with a dusty window, and a door that led into the yard. This Withers ascertained right away.

'It's jest a matter o' slipping round the corner to get to the window of Jackman's room,' he said. He turned to Hank and Pete: 'We'd better give the place a thorough going-over.'

While the philosophic Carlo stood by with a seemingly perpetual shrug, and Pellow lingered meekly just inside the curtain, the three men turned drawers upside down and ferreted among cutlery, dug to the depths of culinary utensils and ransacked cupboards.

A slicker hung on a hook on the back door. Pete dug into the deep pockets of this and, at the second attempt came forth with a Colt .45. He spun the cylinder.

'There's one shot bin fired,' he said. He sniffed at it. 'Not so long ago, either,' he added.

Carlo forgot his philosophic attitude and waddled forward beaming nervously.

'That your gun?' growled Withers.

'Ah, yes,' said Carlo. 'Weeth that one bullet I shot a carrion crow who had been comin' around ze back for weeks.'

Withers' eyes squinted. 'Yeh?' He turned to Pellow. 'You know anythin' about this.'

'Yes, Carlo told me about the crow,' said the manager.

'But you didn't know he'd shot it?'

'No.'

'Helluva story,' said Withers half to himself. He turned on Carlo.

'Ah suppose you didn't know your boss was shot with a forty-five – we dug the slug out o' the wall in the office.'

'Ah – no.'

'Ah guess ah'll have to take you in,' said Withers.

'No,' said Carlo, quivering, his little eyes shining with terror. 'I know nothink about it. I love ze boss.'

'C'mon,' said Withers roughly.

'Better come along quietly, Carlo,' said Hank.

Carlo saw an opening and suddenly made a dash for the back door. For all his bulk he was surprisingly quick. But Pete forestalled him with a carefully placed foot. Carlo tripped over this and went head-first into the door with a sickening crash. They helped him to his feet, a quivering, blubbering mass of flesh. Then he went quietly.

Hank and Pete were in their room later that night.

'D'yuh think the greaser did shoot Jackman?' said Pete.

'It certainly looks thataway,' said Hank. 'Anyway, the marshal had every right to hold him on the evidence.'

'Could such a blubberin' coward do a job like that tho'?'

'It doesn't take a lot o' guts to shoot a man in the back. Yes, I guess Carlo did do it an' was too scared, and in too much of a hurry to get back in his kitchen to stay an' make sure he did the job properly.'

'An' yet Carlo, altho' he's scared to death, won't tell who paid him to do the job. He keeps sayin' he knows nothin' about it.'

'Maybe he's too scared to tell.'

'Surely he'd tell to save his own neck?'

'Maybe nobody paid him. Maybe it was all his own idea. Maybe he had some grudge against Jackman. They do say Jackman has a nasty way with his men.'

'Maybe…. Altho' Withers seems to think this attempted murder o' Jackman is tied up with the other murders, an' the man who's behind them all hired Carlo to do this one.'

Hank's leathery brow was more furrowed than usual. He did not answer right away. When he did he said:

'Yuh know – for a bit I kinda suspected Jackman might've had somep'n to do with the murders himself….'

'Yeh, I'd thought o' that, too,' said Pete. 'He seems to be the sort of man who'd go to any lengths for money and power.'

'If we work on the assumption that the people behind the other murders tried to get Jackman, too, wal, I guess that washes Jackman out as a suspect. But if on the other hand we figure the attempted murder o' Jackman had nothin' to do with the other jobs, Jackman remains on the list.'

'Even so, we're not much further ahead.'

'Nope. I guess not.'

'Fancy pair o' private investigators we turned out tuh be,' said Pete with a disgruntled grin.

'Never mind, son,' said Hank. 'The marshal's gonna interview Jackman first thing tomorrow morning if the big-shot's all right. Maybe we'll learn some'p'n else then.'

Pete did not seem very convinced.

TEN

They were up bright and early the following morning and in next to no time having breakfast served to them at the corner table by the omnipresent Perce. There it was Withers found them when he came lumbering in, his big, flabby face glistening with sweat, his breath coming in gasps.

The partners eyed him with surprise.

'Jackman's gone,' he gasped as soon as he could get his words out.

'Gone!' echoed the partners.

Pete followed up with: 'Wal, maybe he's gone back to his ranch.'

'He promised to see me in my office this mornin',' said the marshal. 'The doc told him not to move.... An' he hasn't gone to his ranch. I've seen Pellow an' he says Jackman took the early stage to Sundown City. Pellow says the only reason he can think of is that he's gone to see his lawyer who hangs out there.'

'Wal, didn't he say anythin' to Pellow 'fore he went?' said Hank.

'No. Pellow, who sleeps there, saw him thru' the window an' saw him get on the stage.'

'He couldn't 'uv been as much hurt as we thought,' said Hank. He rose to his feet. 'Somethin' smells mighty fishy to me. Let's all go an' see Pellow.'

They left their breakfast and went and saw Pellow, but he only told the same story over again. He was agitated and incoherent and, if he wasn't tellin' the truth, at least he was a darned good actor.

Hank crossed to Jackman's office and opened the door.

'Couldn't we give this place a going-over and see if we could find anythin'?' he said.

'No – please,' bleated Pellow.

'No, Ah guess we couldn't do that, Hank,' said Withers gravely. 'Jackman might've gone to Sundown City on some legitimate business on the spur of the moment. We've got nothin' against him. Ah guess we ain't got the rights to do anythin' like that – with Mr Pellow here as witness an' all.'

'Guess you're right,' said Hank, turning away.

It was a moody trio who let the Koh-i-nor Eating House: the partners going back to the Palace to finish their breakfast, the marshal returning to the jail and his prisoner.

We'll be with you in about half-an-hour, marshal,' said Hank. 'An' we'll work on that greaser till his eyes drop out.'

'All right,' said Withers lumbering off.

Carlo, the cook, sat on the end of the low bunk with his head down, his fat shoulders humped, his hands hanging down between his legs. He did not look up when Hank and Pete entered the cell.

Hank spoke his name. He looked up then, his eyes scared, his whole manner cringing as if he expected to be beaten.

'Nobody's gonna hurt you, Carlo,' said Hank, 'as long as you're reasonable.'

'I didn't keel the boss, meester,' said the cook.

'Mebbe yuh didn't,' said Hank. 'The marshal's only holdin' you on suspicion, yuh know. You must admit the evidence is purty thick. Jackman was shot at with a Colt .45 an' we find one in your pocket with one slug missin' – you even admitted it was your gun.'

'It was,' said Carlo, dully. 'I shot that slug at a pestilent carrion crow.'

'An' did yuh hit him?'

'Yes, I keeled him.'

'What did yuh do with the carcass?'

'I buried it.'

'Now we're gettin' someplace,' said Hank. 'Was the slug still in the body when you buried it'

'I theenk so.'

'Where did you bury it?'

Carlo's eyes brightened, he sat up straighter. 'I buried heem at the bottom of the rubbish-heap right opposite my keetchen door.'

'All right, Carlo, that'll do for now,' said Hank.

As they left the cell Carlo called out. 'I deed not keel my boss. You will prove, *senores*....'

'Maybe,' said young Pete softly. He turned to Hank. 'Wal, we didn't give him the workin'- over we told Withers we would. Still I gotta hand it tuh yuh, old-timer, we certainly discovered some'p'n— Or did we?'

'That remains to be seen,' said Hank. 'I only thought o' that angle at the last moment.'

'Where to now?'

'The Koh-i-nor, I guess, said Hank.

They entered the office and told the marshal of their intentions. Like a cautious old steer he munched and stamped a little, muttering something about 'private prop- erty,' but finally was persuaded to accompany them.

At the Koh-i-nor Eating House Pellow greeted them nervously. He seemed relieved to learn he was not wanted

for another cross-examination and gladly supplied them
with spades.

They passed through the kitchen, where one of the
establishment's gangling youths was deputising for Carlo.
'Go back into the dining-room, son,' Withers told him.
'An' stay there till we come back.'

The youth gaped, then disappeared through the
curtain. Withers opened the door and led the way to the
rubbish heap.

'Looks like the ground's bin disturbed here,' said Pete
jabbing the spot with his spade. The implement sank into
the soft soil. He drove it in further with his foot then
heaved.

'I think I've got it,' he said.

Hank joined him and shovelled a few spadefuls away.

Pete brought the carcase of the bird to the surface. It
was just beginning to decompose.

'It ain't bin here long,' said Hank.

Pete split he carcase open with the sharp edge of his
spade. Something glittered among the feathers, blood and
bones. Gingerly the young man picked it out. He straightened up and held it in the palm of his hand.

'That's a .45 slug all right,' said Hank. He took it from
Pete's hand. 'It's marked badly,' he said. 'I don't think the
one we took from Jackman's office was marked thataway,
was it, marshal?'

Withers took the slug and inspected it. 'I don't remember it bein' marked,' he said. 'We can soon find out.
'C'mon.'

They followed him back to the office.

He unlocked the front door with his key and led them
inside.

'Ah put the slug in mah drawer,' he said. 'An' Carlo's
gun with it.'

He squeezed his huge bulk between the desk and his

chair and squatting down, opened the drawer,

'Here's the gun.' He tossed it on the desk.

'All right,' said Hank.

Withers rummaged about in the drawer. 'The pesky thing's got stuck in a corner or somep'n I reckon,' he said.

Withers began to take everything out of the drawer and put on the desk. Papers, reward notices, pens and pencils, gummed labels, a box of cartridges, a bowie-knife in its sheath, and other miscellaneous articles, all jumbled together.

They grubbed in silence for a while, sorting out the papers and putting the smaller objects to one side. Finally Hank said: 'It doesn't seem tuh be here, marshal.'

'But it's got to be,' expostulated Withers, perspiring freely. 'Ah put it in here with the gun. I know I did.'

He got down on his hands and knees, and began to rummage under and around the desk. Any other time the sight of this huge man crawling about like a baby grizzly would have raised smiles. But in this case Pete and Hank were peeved about the disappearance of an important clue; their faces remained sober and rather grim.

Finally, puffing and perspiring, Withers lumbered to his feet.

He smiled sheepishly. 'Maybe Ah put it in a safe place in mah quarters.'

The marshal's 'quarters' as he called them were in the back of the office. He led the way through a door beside the locked one that led into the jail.

It was the first time the partners had been in the marshal's private place. They looked around them with interest as they stood in the living-room.

'Three rooms,' mumbled Withers. 'Bedroom an' small kitchen in back.'

The living-room was largish and comfortable. A massive oak dining-table stood dead in the centre with four dining-chairs grouped around it. There were two comfortable armchairs, a massive oak sideboard and a tall bookcase. This latter was half-full of books, which looked however as if they had not been touched for years.

Beside the bookcase was a small bureau. Over the bureau hung a sabre in its scabbard. There were three or four pictures on the dark-papered walls. The floor was bare dark-stained boards, but it was almost entirely covered by rush mats and one or two skins.

The place was dignified, almost sombre, but very tidy.

'That table an' the sideboard belonged to my maw,' mumbled Withers. 'Ah shouldn't like to part with them…. The place has been like this ever since I became marshal here,' he explained. 'An old dame from down the street comes an' does it for me every week. In the beginnin' Ah used to have lots o' guests – but I don't bother now. Ah don't spend much time here now, an' I eat out most o' the time.' Suddenly he seemed to recollect what brought them there and, lumbering over to the bureau, opened it and began to rummage industriously inside.

Hank stood behind him and gazed up at the sabre on the wall. The marshal turned his head.

'I was in a cavalry regiment when Ah was a young man,' he said, with almost boyish pride.

The marshal calmed down and became more methodical in his search. He went through the bureau thoroughly, but failed to find anything remotely resembling a .45 slug. Hank, watching every move, figured that, judging by the dusty and aged appearance of some of the articles and papers in the bureau, it had not had such a through going-over for years.

Withers turned again. 'What can have happened to it?'

'Go thru' all your pockets again,' said Hank.

Withers complied, but without any luck.

'Has anybody bin here this mornin'?' Hank asked him.

'No…. Oh, yes! Sam Fernicutt called in first thing.'

'Oh,' said Hank. 'An' did yuh tell him about the gun an' the slug we got out of Jackman's office.'

'Yeh,' said Withers. 'Ah didn't see any harm in it. He'd heard about us jailin' Carlo an' he wanted to know about the case…. We bin pards for a good many years.'

'Maybe,' said Hank. 'But don't forget Pellow said he suspected Fernicutt of havin' a hand in pluggin' his boss. Carlo ain't bin found guilty yet yuh know – if we found that slug it might help to prove he's innocent. Maybe Fernicutt took the slug…. Did yuh show it him?'

'No,' said Withers. 'An' he couldn't ha' took it. He was sittin' right opposite me all the time. He didn't stay long. He just called in on his way out of town.'

'Did he say where he was goin'?'

'No – o, he didn't…. Aw, Ah don't suspect Sam at all,' said the marshal. 'Maybe – maybe somebody got in while we wuz over at the Koh-i-nor.'

'The place was locked up wasn't it?'

'Yeh.'

'Wal, we're doin' no good standing about here. We….'

'Carlo!' interupted Pete suddenly, almost shouting.

'We never looked at Carlo. Maybe somebody got in the back-way.'

'They'd have a job to get thru' that back door,' said Withers. 'Still, we'll go an' have a look…. Ah hope nothin's happened to Carlo.'

But nothing had; they found him fast asleep on his bunk.

ELEVEN

The three of them called in at Pete McCabe's barber shop, which stood right opposite the jail, and made discreet enquiries. But Pete hadn't seen anybody mosyin' around the jail at all that morning since he'd seen Sam Fernicutt call first thing.

That afternoon young Pete meandered off to make enquiries all on his lonesome. His quest led him up to the other end of town. What he expected to discover there was hard to say. It was the quieter corner with little cabins where some of the oldest settlers, the fathers of 'Diablo' lived. And shops too. A hardware shop, a grocers, Tod Bentley's famous boot shop, the small confectioner's where 'the girls' got their candy. And Stella Dempsey's draper's shop.

Just before he reached Stella's Pete passed Sam Fernicutt on foot.

'Howdy.' said the saloon-owner.

'Howdy,' answered Pete mechanically. He was surprised to see Fernicutt. He figured it had not taken the saloon-owner long to get back from his trip. Still, maybe he hadn't been far. Or maybe he hadn't been at all – the nearest town, Sundown City, was over a day's ride away.

Don Miguel Carmenito's hacienda was almost that, too, by all accounts. Ep Jackman's ranch was the only other place at all near, and Fernicutt would hardly go there. Or would he....?

Pete had almost eliminated the saloon-owner's name from his mental list of suspects – despite Pellow's suspicions, and the fact of Fernicutt's visit to the marshal that morning.

But now Pete's suspicions were aroused again. You never knew where you were with these poker-faced gambling sort of ginks!

He entered the shop to find Stella behind the counter. She looked up, startled.

'Oh, it's you, Pete.'

In the last few days they had become great friends and now called each other by their Christian names.

Stella looked disturbed. Pete had an idea why and, without stopping to think, blurted out: 'Has Fernicutt been here?'

'Yes,' said Stella, surprised.

Pete crashed on. 'Has he bin pestering yuh?'

'No, he hasn't been pestering me, Pete,' said Stella, quietly. 'But he did ask me to marry him.... This is the sixth time,' she added with a little smile.

'An' did you accept him this time?'

Stella's lips quirked again. 'Well, if it's any business of yours, Pete Henderson, I didn't. But I might get around to changing my mind.... Have you got anything against Sam Fernicutt?'

'No – o, I guess not. But....'

'But what?'

'I dunno....'

'Pete,' Stella's voice became suddenly very serious. 'You don't think Sam Fernicutt had anything to do with those horrible crimes? With the death of – my father?'

'I don't know what to think, Stella,' said Pete miserably.

He told her of the events that had happened, of the way Fernicutt seemed to be tied up with all of them. Stella also did not know what to think. Her manner made Pete wonder whether she considered him a little prejudiced against the suave saloon-man. Maybe he was just imagining things – he was getting sensitive all of a sudden. Why did this girl make him that way.... Yeh, maybe he was prejudiced. He felt impelled to change the subject and burst out with:

'I'm plumb throwed an' hog-tied, Stella.' Then because his vehemence seemed to startle her a little he added reflectively. 'But I guess Hank has got plenty of ideas. He usually has but he won't tell 'em anybody – not even me – until he's got som'p'n concrete to build 'em on. He's a canny ole buzzard is Hank.'

'I like him,' said the girl impulsively. 'But he puzzles me. I don't think he's really as gruff and hard-bitten as he pretends to be. He's never spoken much to me – at times he seems to ignore me. There's somethin' about him – I dunno – something kind of sad I think....'

'Something happened years ago,' said Pete.

'What?' said Stella, her feminine curiosity awakened.

Before he could stop himself Pete had blurted it out. 'He got hurt badly by the gel he married. She was no good. Her name was Stella like yours.'

A spasm of pain crossed the girl's face. Pete could have bitten his tongue off. Impulsively he reached across the counter and caught hold of her hands.

'I yap on an' on like a prairie-dog,' he said. 'I ought to keep my mouth shut. An' when I said her name was Stella like yours I didn't mean anything. I mean I didn't....'

She smiled at him understandingly. The next moment he had drawn her closer to him and was kissing her. Her lips were warm, soft and yielding. He let go of her hands and clasped her firm warm shoulders. Then he let her go suddenly and stood away.

'I'm sorry, Stella,' he said.

Her head was lowered. 'Are you?' she said tonelessly. She turned abruptly without showing him her face. She went through the door behind her into the back and left him gaping. He stood uncertainly for a moment then, with a shrug of his broad shoulders opened the outer door and went out. The bell clanged shrilly. He closed the door gently behind him.

But he kicked stones like a petulant kid as he walked down the street. Whether Stella was offended with him or not he did not know. She had not seemed unduly het-up. Maybe she had wanted him to follow her into the back. Women were certainly hard to figure. He'd never had a great lot to do with them....

Having Hank for a pard, imbibing the oldster's subtle unspoken antagonism towards the opposite sex, had made Pete mighty leary of the whole passel of 'em. It was ironical that the woman who Pete had perhaps taken the most interest in should bear the same name as the one who had done Hank wrong.... Stella! Pete cursed under his breath and kicked another stone viciously. If he didn't watch himself he was liable to get himself roped, hog-tied and branded before he could bat his baby-blue eyes. Would that be bad? Hell....!

He was getting into the busier part of the main drag. People glanced at him curiously. The dark young stranger looked kind of peeved about something. If they had not already seen him in action they knew of his exploits. They got out of his path and left him severely alone.

He was getting near to the Palace when he heard the babble. He forgot his moody speculations and looked ahead. There was something going on outside the saloon. As he got nearer Pete saw the top of Jonathan Helliwell's prairie-schooner.

One of the canvas sides of the waggon was rolled back, leaving an improvised platform with a small counter. On the counter were rows of bottles filled with brightly-coloured liquid of various shades. There were piles of pretty-looking tins and boxes too. Helliwell certainly believed in colour.

The medicine-man had a bottle in his hand. He held it up. The green liquid it contained shone brightly in the sunlight. It flashed when he moved it.

At one end of the counter stood the little, yellow-faced Bicker. In the shadows of the mysterious inner sanctum of the waggon loomed the figure of big Jack.

Helliwell held the bottle in the palm of one hand and slapped it with the other.

'I repeat, my friends,' he boomed. 'This is the finest salve, embrocation and lotion on the market. A hundred-purpose liquid, my friends, as I am prepared to prove. Is there any gentleman or lady in the crowd who has, by some fell chance, acquired a severe blister, a burn, an abrasion or a wound of any kind? I....'

A screechy female voice interrupted him. 'Hey, mister! Biddy here fell on the stove this mawnin' an' burnt her knee.'

'Aw, cut-it out,' shrilled another female voice, presumably belonging to Biddy. 'I don't want no nuthin' on my knee. I don't want anybody messin' around with my knee....'

Biddy was hustled to the front. Despite her shrill protests she had obviously entered into the spirit of the joke now. She was a blowzy, dance-hall girl with dirty yellow hair.

She leered up at Helliwell. 'I don't believe the stuff's any good at all,' she said.

'Good fer you, Biddy.' 'You tell him, gel.' 'Do yer stuff, medicine-man.' The crowd were right behind her now.

Helliwell boomed. 'If the little lady will step into my parlour and I will be happy to oblige.'

There were a few titters. 'Don't you trust him, Biddy,' yelled a female voice.

There were more cries and laughter. Helliwell ignored them. He spoke to Bicker.

The little man got down from the waggon. He advanced gravely to the girl and took her arm. He led her to the step. From up above Helliwell helped her up. The crowd watched silently. Biddy was obviously at a loss now. She faltered a little, she looked from side to side as if seeking escape.

But Helliwell, irrespective of his reactions in the first place, meant to go through with it now. There were whistles and cheers from the crowd as he persuaded Biddy to put her leg up on a cleared spot on the low counter.

The girl's legs were definitely her best item. Helliwell spoke to her again and she simpered coyly.

'Go it, Biddy,' yelled the crowd. 'Show the gennelman yore knee.'

'Cmon, Biddy,' shouted one bull-like voice. 'Yuh know you've got the best legs in Diablo.'

Well, after that, what could the girl do? She'd meant to do it all along anyway.

She pulled her skirt up above her knee. The member was bandaged. With deft fingers Helliwell undid the knot. The crowd cheered frenziedly. The medicine-man bowed, but without a smile.

'The young lady has a very nasty burn on her beautiful white knee,' he said. 'But I'll soon fix that.'

He held the bottle of green stuff aloft again. 'With a small application of my wonder lotion I will heal the little lady's wound.'

Big Jack handed him a pad of cottonwool. He soaked it with the lotion then applied it to Biddy's sore spot. The crowd watched silently and in admiration. Biddy giggled.

The crowd cheered. 'Go it, medicine-man.' 'How's he makin'-out, Biddy?' 'Have him do it again tonight, Biddy.'

Even as their cries died down again and they watched Helliwell produce fresh bandage and lint another diversion occurred.

A thick hoarse voice bawled: 'You leggo o' my gel's leg!'

A big tow-headed young man had come out of the Palace and was swaying on his feet in the dust just off the boardwalk.

'It's Big Harry, Biddy's man,' screeched a female.

'He's as jealous as a bobcat,' said another one.

The girl on the waggon turned her head to look at the drunken man. 'Harry,' she said, 'I....'

'Leggo of her,' bawled the man hoarsely. He drew his gun and waved it, to the menace of everybody in the street.... 'Leggo!'

Helliwell let the girl go. She screamed, pushed past Bicker and dropped from the waggon.

'My friend,' said Helliwell.

'You dirty son,' bawled Big Harry. 'I'll plug yuh....'

The crowd scattered. Harry's gun boomed. The slug whined harmlessly into the air above the prairie-schooner. The condition Big Harry was in he couldn't hit a target. But he was still mighty dangerous. He was squinting, levelling his gun for another shot, ignoring the Derringer in Helliwell's hand – he probably didn't see it anyway.... A black-haired young man leapt from the crowd and tackled him around the body. The gun went off again, shattering an upstairs window in the Palace. Then, mouthing hoarse curses Big Harry was grappling with his attacker. His gun was sent spinning away from him. The attacker stood away too. Growling deep in his throat Big Harry charged. The dark young man measured him as he came on then hit him flush in the middle of his beefy face. Harry's heels left the ground. He might have been kicked by a steer – the effect was the same. His back hit the dust with such force that it seemed to send a ripple along the street. He lay still.

'Harry,' Biddy ran screeching from the crowd and went on her knees beside him.

'He'll be all right, ma'am,' said Pete Henderson. He looked up at the waggon. 'Carry on, Mr Helliwell,' he said.

The medicine-man bowed gravely. 'Thank you, my young friend,' he said, then as if nothing had happened, he went on with his spiel.

Pete looked around him challengingly at the re-forming crowd. But nobody wanted to take matters up where Big Harry had left off. They had seen this dark, devil-may-care younker in action against Piute Joe and Big Tom Lowrie the other night. Both these gunmen were now comfortably everlastingly rested in Boot Hill. And now Big Harry. He was lucky to only get his face mussed-up. The hard-boiled denizens of Diablo left Pete Henderson well alone. Right now, anyway....

Pete turned. He felt good. He had forgotten all about Stella Dempsey.

He entered the Palace. Hank was coming down the stairs.

'What's all the shootin' about?' he said. 'You bin gettin' in trouble again, yuh young skunk?'

'Nothin' tuh worry about, ol'-timer,' said Pete airily. They breasted the bar. 'Set 'em up, Perce,' said Pete.

After that it was a race between them. While they got pickled on snake-poison it was as if there had never been a gel named Stella – for both of them!

After dinner they had a snooze. Pete woke with a brilliant shaft of sunshine spearing through the window and beating on his face. He rose with a yawn and a grimace. He felt fuggy. Hank was still snoring. Even with his mouth wide open he looked kind of peaceful.

Pete figured he'd go out and have a ride to clear his head.

Pete donned the necessary; characteristically, taking more time over the hang of his guns than anything else. He stole from the room. Hank's snores floated after him and died away as he descended the stairs. Pete tried a 'hair of the dog' quickly with Perce then went out to the stables and saddled-up. A few minutes later he took the trail out of town.

At the same time Hank McDonald awoke with a groan and rolled over.

'Pete,' he said.

No answer. Pete's place was empty. 'Probably downstairs soakin' himself again,' growled Hank aloud. He climbed laboriously off the bed and began to put on his boots.

When he got downstairs Perce told him that Pete had gone out riding 'jest for a blow'.

Hank had a drink with the taciturn barman then took another one over to a corner table. The saloon was almost empty. Two girls were giggling in another corner. Three men were playing poker. A morose-looking cowboy sat drinking alone. Hank found a pack of cards and began to play solitaire.

He looked up instinctively as another arrival entered the saloon. He was a young man, well-made, lithe, of medium build, his face dark and saturnine. As he crossed the boards to the bar he reminded Hank of a mountain lion stalking his prey. He covertly followed him with his eyes. Perce turned around from glass-polishing and saw the newcomer.

The look on the barman's face was mighty interesting to the old-timer. It showed surprise, almost disbelief, and there was a shifty quality in the little eyes that was hard to figure. That Perce knew the guy well was evident. But he hadn't been expecting him, he was almost shocked to see him; whether they were friends or otherwise was hard to determine.

Perce's face reassumed its usual doughy look.

'Hi-yuh, Uck,' he said.

The other's voice was deep and low but it carried to Hank in the corner.

'Hi-yuh, Perce. How's tricks?'

'So-so. You?' Perce pushed a bottle of whiskey and a glass across the bar.

'I'm makin' out,' said the other as he poured himself a stiff tot. He shoved the bottle back to Perce. 'Have one.'

Perce took one. They watched each other as they drank. The by-play seemed a little strained.

Hank had no difficulty in sensing this fact. Also he noted what effect the new arrival's entrance had on the other occupants of the saloon. The percentage-girls had quit their giggling, the poker-players were turning to look. Only the morose young cowboy, who was half-soused anyway, paid no attention to anything but the moisture in the bottom of his glass. He staggered to his feet and from his end of the bar growled: 'Whip one along hyar, Perce.'

With a flick of his wrist he sent the empty glass whistling along the bartop. Drunk or not his aim was pretty good. He followed the glass with a coin. Perce caught them both expertly, filled the glass and spun it back. The cowboy caught it, grunted surlily and plonked it down on his table. He slumped once more into his chair.

Everybody had been watching this little act so what happened next came as a surprise to all. One of the men at the poker-table rose suddenly, a gun in his hand. It was pointed at the dark man at the bar.

'Up with 'em, Uck!'

At the other's barked command Uck turned and faced him. A sudden tension of his whole body was the only sign of surprise that he showed.

'Careful, Uck,' said the poker-player. 'One funny move an' you're a dead man. Up with 'em I said.'

Slowly the dark man raised his hands. 'Howdy, Mike,' he said.

Mike was dark too, very thin and pale. He wore black store-clothes and looked like a gambler. He kicked his chair away from him and advanced on the other.

'I've been wantin' to meet up with you ever since you got Joe Santos, you back-shootin' snake.'

The other's lips quirked but he looked as inscrutable as an Indian. He said: 'Joe Santos asked for it. Ain't no call for you to take it up.'

'You say,' said the other. 'But that's just what I am doing. I ain't gonna give you a chance to gut shot me an' I ain't stirring up no passel o' trouble jest for you. I'm figuring the marshal 'ull be mighty glad to see you. That's where you're goin'. Move away from that bar….!' His voice rose and suddenly: 'Keep your hands still, Perce, keep 'em on top there – I ain't takin' no chances.'

The man they called Uck turned full around to face his captor as he moved away from the bar.

His well-worn black long-sleeved short coat swung open and, for the first time, Hank McDonald saw the coloured shirt the man wore. It was a real bobby-dazzler; a brilliant green with red stripes in a check pattern. Although the old-timer had never seen a shirt like that before he figured maybe he'd seen a piece of cloth that corresponded with it. He wondered whether that shirt had a piece torn from it somewhere beneath that coat. He'd said it before and he'd say it again: surely there couldn't be two shirts like that in the territory. If there was it was a dadblamed coincidence—

Hank felt like jumping up and ripping the man's coat from his back to make sure. But he held his horses. Now was no time to show his hand. He awaited developments.

Mike, the man with the gun, was rapping out harsh commands. 'Walk towards the door! Walk I said!'

Uck veered a little. The drunken cowboy was taking an interest in the proceedings now. He watched the movement of both men with owlish eyes, his mouth hanging slackly open. His chair scraped as he lurched to his feet, wagging his finger at Uck. 'I know you,' he burbled.

Mike was half-turning, surprised. Uck acted, covering the ground in one leap, his fist rising and falling. Clipped viciously on the side of the jaw, Mike crashed to the floor and rolled. His gun fell from his hands. He lay on his back, reaching for it. Uck drew and fired. Mike screamed as his clutching hand was smashed by the heavy slug which went right through and bit into the boards beneath it.

A chair crashed over as another man rose at the poker-table. Uck whirled, firing again. The man clutched at his shoulder and cursed in agony. His gun hit the table-top, slid and hit the floor with a dull thud.

Uck had both guns out now and was backing up towards the door. His face seemed darker, his eyes glowed, his lips were stretched in a vicious grimace.

'Take it easy everybody,' he said.

His guns covered the room as he cat-footed backwards to the batwings. Hank McDonald smiled thinly. He'd certainly like to get acquainted with this fast-shooting hombre who Marshal Withers would like to see and who wore such a pretty shirt.

The batwings parted, Uck backed through them and out of sight. His boot-heels thudded then the sound faded.

Hank McDonald cleared the room in a few strides and passed through the side-door into the alley. His passage was swift down the tunnel-like cutting. He stopped at the end, flattening himself against a board-wall. He peered around the corner. His surmise had been correct. To make his getaway Uck had taken to the backs. As Hank watched the dark man half-turned abruptly and disappeared.

The old-timer took a chance and turned the corner. His hand was on his gun. Uck may have seen him. He might be waiting in cover up there. Hank moved along warily, keeping close to the walls, using all the cover he could, passing ash cans and rubbish, and sagging back doors. He reached the point where his quarry had disappeared, the back of a one-storey frame building. There was one grimy window and a door from which the once-brown paint was peeling. Hank looked around him, drew the gun. Then he tried the door.

It opened. He slid through the aperture into the comparative gloom beyond. There was no sound. He took a step forward. Then the roof seemed to fall on his head. Curses rose to his lips but were never uttered as he plunged sickeningly into oblivion.

When he came to he lay for a moment fighting off the nausea that made him feel weak and ill. He was a tough old bird and this wasn't the first time he had been knocked out – his cranium had survived worse bashings than this one. He was too canny to open his eyes and start up right off in case his assailant was still watching him. He opened them the merest crack. He couldn't see anybody. He listened. There didn't seem to be anybody around. He opened them wide and sat up. It was as he'd figured: the mangy skunk had hightailed it. Hank cursed himself now for walking into the trap. The other had gotten clean away and the old-timer's curiosity was still unsatisfied. He rose to his feet, teetering a little. He took a deep breath. He gazed around him, feeling his head ruefully where a size-able lump was forming.

He was in a kitchen. There was a small iron pump in the corner; an oil-stove; a cupboard; a small deal-table and one rickety chair. There was a smell of stale grease. The place looked as if it hadn't been used for a long time.

There was another door. Feeling almost as good as new again, and still curious, Hank crossed to the door and opened it. He went through into a larger room – an office with an old roll-top desk, filing cabinets round the walls, a few chairs. The place smelled musty. Hank crossed to the desk. It was not locked. He lifted the lid. There was nothing there at all except a sprinkling of dust that had gotten through the top. He tried the drawers, they were empty too. So were the filing cabinets.

This was just a disused office; very convenient for Uck's little slugging act.

Hank passed through another door into a small bare annexe, the sort lots of offices have. A dusty window looked out upon the street.

Hank looked through just as Marshal Withers was passing by. The old-timer grabbed the front door, cursed when it would not open, drew the bolt, dashed out calling: 'Marshal.'

Withers turned, surprise written all over his moon-like face.

'There's bin a ruckus at the Palace,' said Hank.

'Yeh, I know,' said Withers. 'I'm jest goin' down there.'

Swiftly Hank told him everything.

They were approaching the batwings of the Palace. Withers said; 'I know of only one guy who could be called Uck. I didn't think that skunk 'ud have the nerve....'

He broke off as they entered the saloon. The little fat doctor was bandaging the shoulder of the wounded man. The black-garbed Mike, his hand already trussed up, was slumped in a chair. Hank noted that the tipsy cowboy, whose actions had precipitated the shooting was no longer there.

Mike looked up as the marshal crossed to him. 'Uriah Le Bruque's bin here,' he said tonelessly. 'I tried to take him....'

'Goddam it!' bawled Withers. 'I had that skunk run outa town months ago.... What did he want?'

'I don't know,' said Mike.

'Perce might be able to tell yuh,' said Hank.

They crossed to the bar But Perce knew nothing. 'Uriah didn't tell me anythin',' he said. 'He didn't have much chance before Mike throwed down on him.'

Withers turned to Hank. 'Le Bruque shot a dealer at Faro Pentecost's casino some months ago. A hombre named Joe Santos. Mike there was his pard. Ah guess Santos didn't have much of a chance. He still got a couple o' cards in his hand when we picked him up, shot thru' the side of his chest. There were so many witnesses for an' against that things looked like b'ilin' up into a feud or something. Finally Ah had Le Bruque run outa town. Ah should like to've had him hanged – but public opinion wuz mixed – don't do to stir up too much strife in a town like this or people'll get kilt in dozens.... Ah ought to've had Le Bruque taken out an' drowned in the crick. He's a bad hombre. Ah never figured he'd have the nerve to come back here. I wish I knew what he wuz after....'

'That office where he dry-gulched me,' said Hank. 'Who does it belong to?'

'The Carmenitos,' said Withers. 'But that don't signify nothin'. They ain't used it for ages.' He paused. 'Tho' now I come to think, Le Bruque did useter work for the Carmenitos. He probably knew it was empty, that's why he used it.'

The two men left the saloon. They hunted for Uriah Le Bruque, but were not surprised that they didn't find him.

They went back to the Palace just as Pete Henderson was returning from his ride. When he heard the news he cursed himself for not being there to see the fireworks –

and maybe take a hand in 'em, too.

'Why, goldarn it,' he burst out. 'I passed a dark hombre out on the trail. Riding a big sorrel.'

'That'd be him I guess,' said Withers.

'We said "howdy" to each other,' said Pete. He threw back his head and went off into peals of laughter. 'If only I'd've known,' he spluttered.

He caught sight of his pardner's morose face. 'It's a sign I didn't stay home tuh play nussmaid t'yuh,' he spluttered.

Hank cursed him fluently and at length. Then he ceased as suddenly as he had begun. 'Did yuh notice his shirt?' he said.

Pete's eyes widened, his mouth dropped open. 'Did I notice his shirt yuh said? Air you plumb loco,' bleated Pete. 'Has getting all het-up an' bothered made yuh lose your senses. Why in tarnation should I notice his shirt?'

'It was a real bobby-dazzler. Green with red stripes.'

'An' yuh kept that little item o' news till last yuh dadblasted ole coyote,' said Withers. 'So it looks like Le Bruque killed Marty.... maybe Clem, too.'

'Maybe,' said Hank non-committally.

The marshal spoke then: 'Yuh mean like young Marty...?'

TWELVE

Marshal Obadiah Withers was a gaming man. He always spent two or three evenings every week in Faro Pentecost's 'gambling-hell' and kept a fatherly eye on things. His presence there had helped to keep the peace in many instances and as the marshal wasn't averse to a flutter himself whilst he was keeping the peace, he was always welcome. In fact he was one of Faro's best customers. Sometimes he won – but most times he lost: nobody can 'buck the tiger' for long and come out on top.

That night he had asked Pete and Hank to meet him there, as he put it: 'Jest to look things over sort of.' The partners did not expect to find any clues in a gambling-hell, but, as Hank said, it would be as well to go there if only to keep an eye on the marshal. Neither of them could figure him out properly, but the incident of the disappearing .45 slug had made them mighty leary. Pete said maybe it was just old age creeping on, and the marshal would happen on the slug sometime when he wasn't looking for it. In some measure Pete proved to be right.

When they met Withers he was beaming all over his fat face. He led them into a dusky corner of the gambling-house and showed them something that winked in the palm of his hand. It was a .45 slug.

'Ah found it right in the corner o' my pants pocket,' he told them. 'Right in the linin' it was. It's a wonder Ah didn't lose the pesky thing – it was workin' its way thru' a leetle hole. S'funny thing, Ah don't remember puttin' it in thet pocket. Still,' he handed the slug to Hank, 'You'd better take care of it this time.'

'That's somep'n anyway,' said Hank.'

But bigger things were to happen before that night was out.

It was about three hours later. Withers was winning while Hank and Pete were both losing a mite when a dishevelled puncher burst into Faro's place.

'Marshal Withers here,' he yelled. 'There's a mob goin' down to the jail. They're gonna lynch the Mexican. Perce, the barman, and Uriah Le Bruque are leading 'em.'

'C'mon, marshal,' said Hank.

'Uriah Le Bruque!' bawled Withers. 'What again? I'll fix that dirty snake proper this time!'

The four men pushed out of the place together.

The puncher said: 'He means to string-up thet Mexican higher'n a kite. He's well-primed an' I think Perce's put him up to it. He says the Mex killed Marty an' all the rest.'

'I never did like that Perce,' said Pete.

'Where do you fit in this, son?' Hank asked the young cowboy.

'Sam Fernicutt sent me to get the marshal,' the puncher said. 'He came out jest after Perce an' the rest of 'em had left. Then he went back to fetch his guns…. I ran right along the back lots. We're in front of 'em now.'

What the puncher said was true, but now they could hear the roar of the mob coming down the street and could even see the first batch of them as they crossed shafts of light thrown from windows.

'Keep tuh the side-walk,' said Withers. 'An' hurry.'

The other three had no difficulty in keeping pace with him as he lumbered along, gasping with every stride.

He let them into the office and straight through into the jail-house and the armoury cupboard. From there he got them a wicked-looking sawed-off shotgun apiece.

'You in on this show, kid?' he said to the cowboy.

'Shore.' The young man took the shotgun and stroked the stock lovingly.

'All right. Watch the back door, will yuh?'

They could hear the roar of the mob clearly now. Carlo the cook called from in his cell. Hank went down to him.

The Mexican's eyes were shining with fear. He had heard the noise too, and he knew what was happening. This was not the first time that animal clamouring had been heard in 'The Devil's Frying-Pan.' Even so Carlo asked Hank the question.

'They're comin' for yuh, Carlo,' the old-timer told him. 'But don't worry, they've got to get us first.' He rejoined the others, and they went out front of the office and stood there, shotguns ready.

They did not have long to wait. Pretty soon the street was full of people, the first rank only about a dozen paces away from them. The roaring had died down to an ominous murmur.

'What can I do for you people?' said Withers. He did not shout but his voice carried. Strangely enough he seemed to be enjoying himself.

One man stepped a little way forward from the crowd. He held a flaming torch aloft. He was medium-built, lithe, dark as an Indian.

'We want the Mexican!' he said.

'Oh, it's you, Uriah Le Bruque,' said Withers. 'Ah oughta fill you full of holes.'

'It wouldn't do yuh any good, marshal,' said the man

calmly. 'My friends here 'ud tear you an' your men tuh pieces.'

'Ah like your gall, Uriah,' said Withers. 'But I promise yuh that if any o' your precious friends make a move I'll get you first.'

'You wouldn't do that, marshal?'

'Wouldn't I…?'

Every head turned at a clattering and a rumbling behind. The mob parted to let a waggon come through. It drew up beside the four men. Three men jumped from its interior. Each had a shotgun.

'Would you be wantin' any help, marshal?' said Jonathan Helliwell, the medicine-man.

'You're mighty welcome, Mister Helliwell,' said Withers.

'Wal, maybe I'll do some trade while I'm here,' said Helliwell. He raised his voice and addressed the crowd: 'If there's any o' you people got blood pressure, fallen arches – or itchy trigger-fingers, I got something here for you!'

At the back of the crowd somebody laughed. Little Bicker foraged out a drum from the depths of the waggon and began to thump it.

Le Bruque had begun to spiel again but the drumming drowned his voice: he stood mouthing like a fish on dry land. Bicker was enjoying himself immensely, his yellow, wizened face wreathed by a huge grin as he banged lustily.

Helliwell stood with his coat open, his thumbs hooked into the armholes of his vest and beamed down at the mob like a benign sky-pilot surveying his devout flock. Beside him stood Big Jack, his own broad, homely pan split in twain by a toothy grin, ringlets of his yellow hair hanging almost into his china-blue eyes, which glowed almost tenderly in the torch-light.

The three medicine-men were taking awful chances up there. Any one of the raging mob was liable to go haywire and start shooting.

Uriah Le Bruque's face was darker than ever with passion. He kept opening his mouth and yelling but nothing could be heard above the steady thumping of the drum.

The drum-beat stopped for a bit. It was not Le Bruque's voice that filled the breach but the bull-like tones of that prince of raconteurs, Jonathan Helliwell.

'Walk up! Walk up!' he boomed. 'See the human hyenas. See the two-legged skunks an' coyotes, the snakes that prance, and the buzzards that waggle their behinds like monkeys....'

The shriller voice of Uriah Le Bruque interrupted his flow of rhetoric.

'Shut yuh trap, funny man, before we drag you down an' lynch you 'stead o' the Mex.'

'Yeh,' yelled a voice in the crowd. 'You talk too much. Come on boys, let's rush 'em.'

'That sounds like friend Perce,' said Hank McDonald.

Marshal Withers raised his voice: 'Ah'm warning yuh. Those of yuh in the front won't get very far.'

Helliwell beamed down from his waggon. He didn't seem to know the meaning of fear. 'Peace, my children,' he said.

Le Bruque looked up at him, his face a darkening mask in the torch-light. 'I'll get you: I'll....'

Helliwell made an imperious motion with a plump hand and the rest of Le Bruque's speech was drowned as Bicker began to thump the drum once more.

The night was bright as day as the mob waved their torches and yelled. Very few of them seemed amused. Each one of them waited for his neighbour to make the first move: every one of them was fearful of that grim line of guns before the sheriff's office.

A man broke from the ranks, staggering into the small

clearing before the covered waggon.

Pete Henderson recognised Big Harry the man he'd had a run-in with the other day in similar, if not so perilous circumstances. Harry was drunk again.

He looked up owlishly at Helliwell, teetering on his heels as he bawled. Helliwell made another motion with his hand and the drum-beats ceased. 'Let the gentleman speak,' said the medicine-man.

'You dirty son! You're the one! You're the one I want. I'll lynch you all on my lonesome. I'll take....' Words failed Harry again and he acted.

It was Big Jack who forestalled him as he went for his gun. Jack swept the drum from before Bicker and, reaching downwards with long arms, bashed it down hard over Harry's head.

Harry's head came right through the torn skin. It was a big drum: it went down well over his shoulders too, pinning his arms to his sides. Jack leapt from the waggon. He was very fast for his bulk. He whipped Harry's gun from its holster and tucked it into his own belt. Then he grasped the drunkard by his shoulders and spun him round. He stepped back a couple of paces, swung his boot and let fly.

As if propelled by a gun Big Harry shot headfirst into the crowd. They scattered right and left, some of them sent spinning. Harry's despairing howl floated up from the midst of them. Some of them, enraged, and bolder than the rest advanced on Jack. But with a single leap he was on the waggon again and out of their each.

A few people in the crowd began to laugh as Big Harry staggered to his feet, his face purple as he tried to extricate himself from the loving embrace of the big drum. Then he bent over and let two men get hold of the side of the drum and pull. The drum moved but Harry went with it: they were inseparable. The laughter was redoubled. But it was coarse and ominous. The sort of laughter that could end in tragedy. Even the little pantomime they had just witnessed could not change most of the crowd from their purpose. It was all part of the sport. It was Uriah Le Bruque who spoke again, voice ringing viciously.

'We got no time for funny men! This is serious business.... Are yuh gonna give us the Mexican, marshal?'

'Why should you want the Mexican, Uriah?' retorted Withers. 'As far as I know you only blowed back into town today. What have you agin the Mexican?'

'My friends here have elected me as spokesman,' said Le Bruque. 'I'm speakin' on behalf of all of 'em.'

Withers laughed. 'Where's Perce?'

There was a scuffle and the pallid-faced barman was thrust forward. He stood blinking in the torch-light, shifting his feet nervously.

'What have you got to say, Perce?' said Withers.

The barman found his tongue.

'That Mexican killed my young pard, Marty, an' I'm fer stringin' him up,' he shouted in a high-pitched voice.

The crowd growled. They surged forward a little. The steady line of shotguns did not waver. Helliwell's two 'boys' stood beside their boss and grinned. Helliwell himself looked supremely indifferent. Withers looked grim now and steady as a rock. Hank's face was expressionless as an Indian's. Pete was smiling lopsidedly, a look of unholy glee in his eyes.

'Can you prove that the Mexican killed Marty?' said Withers at length.

Perce almost screeched. 'He killed Marty an' he killed all the others. String him up.'

String him up!' roared the crowd.

'Are yuh gonna fetch him for us or do we have to come an' get him?' yelled Uriah Le Bruque.

'Rush 'em,' yelled somebody at the back.

Withers spoke quietly to Pete as he passed him the keys. 'Go an' let the Mex out and give him a gun. We'll give him a fightin' chance. If we lose he'll be able to turn the gun on himself. It might all be bravado, but you can never tell with these mobs – especially with a devil like Uriah there leadin' 'em.'

Pete went.

He returned and, slinking behind him with another shotgun, came Carlo.

The crowd roared and surged at the sight of him. Pete figured maybe it was a mistake to bring him out. Like letting the dog see the bone, then trying to prevent him from getting it. Still, it was too late now.

'Keep shootin', Carlo,' he said. 'An' make a break if you can.'

'Si,' said the Mexican. He was unnaturally calm now.

The crowd surged and growled. The first ranks came a little nearer.

'Hold it,' yelled a voice at the back.

Heads turned; the mob gaped upwards at the three bedroom windows of Pete McCabe's barber shop. At the centre larger window stood McCabe himself. Twin-barrels of his shotgun gleamed. McCabe had not always been a barber. In his younger days he was marshal of lawless Tombstone for a spell. He was used to mobs.

Beside him stood Sam Fernicutt. The flickering torch-light winked on his levelled six-guns.

Framed in another window so that they almost filled it were McCabe's two strapping sons. They had twin-guns apiece and they looked as if they could use 'em.

At the third and last window stood Emma, their mother, middle-aged, comely, a hard-bitten frontiers woman. She held a repeating rifle in the crook of her arm. And she could shoot as good as any man there – maybe better than most!

The mob became still, muttering.

Sam Fernicutt shouted: 'Listen to me, all of yuh.... Have I ever given you a bum steer?'

There were murmurs of 'No, no.'

'An' I'm not givin' yuh one now,' continued Fernicutt. 'Take heed o' Marshal Withers – he knows what he's talkin' about. If he says the Mexican ain't guilty – well, maybe he ain't....'

The crowd growled at this.

'Wait a minute, ' yelled Fernicutt. 'None of you have an atom o' proof that the greaser is guilty. You've just listened to a couple of *hombres* who say he is. One of 'em used to work for me – well he don't any longer. He's thru. That's what *I* think of his opinion. Marshal Withers has been a good lawman here,' said Fernicutt. 'He ain't poked his nose in everybody's business an' he ain't tried to start a Sunday School. But he has tried to the best of his ability, tuh see that justice is done.... If the greaser's guilty the marshal 'ull see that he hangs....'

'Yuh're durn tootin', Sam,' bawled Withers from the other side of the road.

'Look at it another way, men,' continued Fernicutt. 'We've got yuh covered from both sides. If anybody starts anythin' a whole lot o' you folks are gonna get hurt.... What've you got to say tuh that, Uriah La Bruque?'

The half-breed shrugged philosophically. 'I guess it's your move, Sam,' he said.

'Everybody go back to my place,' he yelled. 'Drinks are on the house.'

That decided it. The crowd began to move back in the direction of the Palace.

The seven men by the jail watched the mob go. Then Withers turned to the Mexican.

'Back to your cell, Carlo,' he said. 'Ah guess that's still the safest place for you.'

The Mexican was trembling now. 'I tell you somethink,

Mister Marshal,' he said. 'I tell yuh....'

'So yuh want to talk now you've nearly got your neck stretched, do yuh?' growled Withers, pushing the man roughly before him. 'Save it till you go inside.'

But Carlo never got inside. He was stopped almost on the doorstep by a heavy slug that almost tore the top off his head. Withers ducked and another slug whisked his hat off. The two reports close together echoed as one. The flash came from the alley beside the barber shop across the street.

Pete was nearest. He drew swiftly and fired in return. Then he ran across the road, weaving, firing as he went. His shots were not answered. Jack and Bicker, Helliwell's two 'boys' followed him as he disappeared in the darkness of the alley.

With guns drawn Helliwell, Withers and Hank McDonald stood over the body of Carlo and watched.

The shouts of the crowd had died away. The street was empty, silent. No more shots were fired.

High heels scraped; four figures appeared at the mouth of the alley. Pete, Bicker, and Jack were returning. With them was Sam Fernicutt.

THIRTEEN

'I bumped into him comin' out of the back door o' the barber's,' said Pete. He sounded a little peeved.

'Yeh,' growled Fernicutt. 'I heard the shots an' came dashing out. When I bumped into him I thought at first he was the hombre who was doin' the shootin'....'

'While we were sortin' ourselves out the other guy got clean away,' said Pete.

'Did yuh see him?'

'Nope! I jest heard him runnin'.'

'What happened?' said Fernicutt.

Withers answered him. 'Somebody bushwhacked us from the alley. He got Carlo – an' he nearly got me. Carlo seemed he was jest gonna spill somep'n too.'

'Too bad,' said Fernicutt. 'If I'd 'uv come out o' that door a bit sooner I'd have caught the hombre who done it....'

'Never mind,' said Withers. 'You've done one good job o' work tonight. We oughta thank you for that.'

'Shore thing,' said Hank.

'Hear, hear,' said Helliwell.

'The barber's the one you gotta thank most,' Fernicutt told them. 'And anyway it didn't help Carlo much in the long run.'

'No, but it helped us. We'd'uv bin gone geese if that mob had rushed us. We couldn't 'uv shot 'em all.'

Helliwell left with his men after Hank, Pete and the marshal had thanked them too, and shaken all three of them by the hand. They mounted the waggon and drove off.

'There goes three white men,' said Pete. 'They'd no call to help us – no cause for to stick their necks out at all – but they did!'

Fernicutt left them and followed the waggon, going back to his establishment and the mob that was having its liquor 'on the house'.

The other three turned then and bent to the grisly task of getting Carlo's body into the office. They covered it with a blanket. Then they called the young cowboy who had faithfully watched the back door all the time.

'That's that,' said Withers. 'Now I've got some business to attend to. Coming, gentlemen?'

The three men followed him out. He locked the door. Here the young cowboy left them swiftly with a muttered 'good-night'.

'I reckon I can guess your business, marshal,' said Hank.

'I reckon yuh can.'

'Yeh, you're after this Uriah Le Bruque.'

'Right.'

'D'yuh figure he's the one who shot Carlo?'

'I wouldn't be surprised,' said the marshal evenly. Anyway – Ah mean tuh shoot him on sight.'

'Who is this Uriah Le Bruque?' said Pete.

'He's an out-an'-out renegade,' said Withers. 'Plain pizen.... I run him out o' town about three months ago after he killed that dealer of Faro Pentecost's in a brawl. If I'd had any sense I'd 'uv killed him then.... Ah won't make the same mistake twice,' he added grimly.

'Does Le Bruque work for anybody in partic'ler?' asked Hank.

'Last I heard of him he was workin' for the Carmenitos,' said the marshal.

'D'yuh think we'll find him at The Palace?'

'Maybe. That's where I'm headin' first.'

The mob there greeted them with cheers, all grudges forgotten, all thought of lynch law dissolved in Fernicutt's liquor.

Withers held up his hands for silence.

'Ah've got somep'n tuh tell you!' he bawled. 'The Mexican got *his* after all.'

There were exclamations of surprise and even incredulity.

'It's the truth Ah'm tellin' yuh!' Withers assured them. 'Somebody fired two shots at us. One missed – the other blew the top of Carlo's haid off…. Does anybody know anythin' about it.'

There was a chorus of 'No's.'

'Is Uriah Le Bruque here?'

'No!'

'Does anybody know where he is?'

Evidently nobody knew this either.

'Maybe Perce can tell yuh,' yelled somebody.

'Where's Perce?'

'He's upstairs packin'…. Perce, Perce,' they began to shout. In their zeal (to keep the law this time) some of them ran upstairs to fetch him.

When they brought him down he was dressed ready to go out, and had his suitcase with him.

'Where's Le Bruque?' barked Withers.

Perce visibly quaked. 'I don't know,' he said. 'He left me in the street.'

'Where did he go?'

'I don't know. He – he jest left.'

'All right,' said Withers. 'Let him thru'…. Where yuh goin' now, Perce?'

'I'm gonna sleep the night at my brother's place,' said the ex-barman. 'Then in the mawnin' I'm gonna take the stage out o' town.'

'Don't ever come back,' said Withers, softly.

'A pretty bunch ain't they?' said Pete as they left.

They enquired after Le Bruque in Faro's place. He had not been there. 'Faro' said he would like to see him – he had a score to settle with that pesky half-breed himself.

They toured the night-spots, even looking in on some of the hole-in-the-corner brothels. But no Le Bruque.

'He musta parked his horse someplace out in the brush,' said Withers. 'He couldn't 'uv planned to stay long.'

'Wal, it certainly looks like he has lit out,' said Pete.

'Yeh, we might as well call it a day,' said Withers. 'But first of all we'd better find Calico Parsons an' tell him we've got another customer for him.'

They found Calico in his rooms in the back of the funeral parlour. They wakened him from a drunken sleep and told him the news. 'All right,' he said, then he grunted, turned over, and went right back to sleep again.

'He won't forget,' said Withers, sardonically. 'He'll be round first thing in the mawnin'. He never forgets a body.'

Before he left the partners he said: 'Ah'm ridin' out o' town in the mawnin' an' I want you boys to look after things here.'

The partners asked no questions.

'All right,' said Hank.

They watched Withers lumber off and then went back to The Palace.

When they got to the office early the following morning Withers had already gone. Pete McCabe called them from his barber's shop. They went over.

He gave them the keys the marshal had left with him. 'Tough about that greaser,' he said.

'Yeh,' said Hank. 'Has Calico called for the body yet?'

'Here he is comin' right now,' said McCabe.

They turned. Calico was driving his one-horse cart in which he fetched the bodies. It was merely a buckboard painted black. The horse, a grey, had a black plume on its forehead.

Pete and Hank went over.

That unsavoury business satisfactorily concluded they split up and went on the prowl, making enquiries, and still keeping a look-out for the elusive Uriah Le Bruque. Although they figured maybe the marshal was riding to take care of that angle.

They met at dinner-time, both confessing they had drawn a blank. In Pete's words: 'Nobody knowed nothin' – or reckoned they didn't.'

'It's a mighty close-mouthed town,' said Hank.

That evening the marshal returned whilst they were in the office. He, too, had drawn a blank.

'I've been across the range,' he told them. 'I've been to Jackman's place, an' I've been to the Carmenitos' hacienda. Le Bruque hasn't been to either place. Ole Don Miguel reckons he sacked Le Bruque some weeks ago an' he ain't seen him since. Le Bruque was a buddy of young José's. Maybe he could've told me somep'n if he'd bin there. But he wasn't....'

'Did Don Miguel say where he was?' asked Hank.

'No, he didn't.'

'How about Jackman? He wasn't back at his ranch was he?'

'Nope. They ain't even heard from him.'

'I saw Pellow today and he ain't heard from him either,' put in Pete.

'There certainly is somep'n queer about Jackman hightailin' it like that,' said Withers. 'Ah wonder where he is now.'

But they were to learn of Jackman's whereabouts sooner than they expected.

Barely five minutes later hooves thundered outside, clattered to a stop; somebody hammered on the outer door.

'Come in,' bawled Withers. He drew his gun and placed it on the desk before him. He was taking no chances.

A travel-stained youth burst into the room. 'Marshal Withers?' he said.

'I'm an express-rider from Sundown City,' the youth panted. 'Lawyer Boniface sent me to tell you Mr Ep Jackman's been shot and killed.'

Withers started from his seat. 'Did they get the one who did it?'

'No, sir, nobody's got any idea who did it. They found Mr Jackman in an alley with a bullet in his back.'

'Had he seen the lawyer first?'

'No, sir. They figured he was on his way to the lawyer's office when he got shot. Marshal Potter of Sundown is workin' on the case. He says he'll get in touch with you. He says maybe there'll be some clues in Jackman's place over here.'

'All right, son,' said Withers.

With an ease born of long practice the youth caught the coin he tossed to him. 'Get goin', son,' said Withers.

After he had gone Withers said; 'Wal, I don't aim to have no other marshal moseyin' about in my territory. If there's any clues here we'll find 'em.' He turned to Hank and Pete. 'I tell you what you can do, boys. It's purty late – go an' give Jackman's office a going-over right now while I have my supper. I ain't had much to eat all day an' Ah'm mighty hungry.'

'Good idea,' said Hank.

'Jest leave it to us, marshal,' said Pete.

They entered Jackman's office by means of the window. They drew the blinds and lit the oil-lamp that hung from the ceiling. Then, working swiftly and almost noiselessly, they began to go over everything. Pete's bowie-knife worked wonders with the locks of the drawers and the cupboard.

They went through countless bills for the sale of cattle, invoices, bills for ranch equipment, armoury; everything straight and above-board. After wading through a particularly large pile of uninteresting papers Pete became exasperated and made more noise than he intended to. Next thing they knew the door had opened and Pellow was covering them with a heavy Colt. He wore a striped night-shirt and slippers.

'Put that gun away you fool,' hissed Hank. 'The marshal sent us…. An' it might interest you to know your boss's been murdered in Sundown City. We're lookin' for somethin' that might help us…. Can you help us?'

Pellow gaped. 'No – o.' he quavered.

Pete went across to him and took the gun from his trembling fingers.

'All right. Vamoose,' he said. 'Get back to bed. An' keep your trap shut.'

Pellow nodded vacantly and scuttled off.

Right at the bottom of the cupboard, in a dusty corner, Pete found something that caused him to emit a startled whistle. He showed the faded sheet of paper to Hank.

'A mortgage!' exclaimed Hank. 'That shore explains a helluva lot. Thet's somep'n the smart hombres did not find – or jest plumb forgot. I guess there's no need to look any further…. Yeh, I guess everything's gettin' linked together nicely now.'

They were crossing the now almost deserted street when two figures ran up to them out of the dark. They drew their guns. Then they recognised the two big sons of Pete McCabe, the barber.

'What the heck....'

'The marshal's bin shot,' panted one. ''He wants you pronto. I reckon he's dyin'. Hurry!'

'Shot!' said Pete. 'Why, we ain't long left him.'

But the two youths were already on their way. 'C'mon.'

They caught up with them. One of them talked as they hurried. 'Dad heard the shot – 'bout five minutes ago. He ran across. He found the marshal in the kitchen. Looks like he's bin shot from the window. Whoever done it got clean away – he had a good start. I think the marshal saw him tho'.... He wouldn't let us fetch the doctor or anythin' – said his number was up anyway. He told us to get you pronto – said he had somep'n important to tell yuh....'

'I figure maybe he has,' said Hank softly.

Obadiah Withers lay on his back on the kitchen floor. McCabe had placed a cushion under his head. He had not risked moving him. It was obvious he was done for. His chest had been shattered by a heavy slug fired at pretty close range.

The kitchen window behind was open.

Withers had lost a lot of blood, but he was not losing it so fast now. His pain was easier. He was dying slowly, gently.

Hank and Pete went on their knees beside him.

'Who did it, marshal?' said Hank softly.

'Uriah Le Bruque,' replied Withers. His voice was subdued but still clear. 'Ah heard him scuffle as he got thru' the window, an' I came runnin' in. He beat me to it.' The marshal paused. Then he said:

'Ah've got a lot to tell you boys an' Ah ain't got much time left. A lot of what Ah'm gonna tell yuh won't be pretty hearin', but I don't want yuh to interrupt. *Sabe?*'

'*Sabe*,' said Hank. 'I guess I know a bit of it. Go on.'

'It all began last year when I borrowed a pile of money from Don Miguel Carmenito to pay some gamblin' debts I owed,' said Withers. 'Don Miguel didn't press me to pay him back until about a fortnight ago, then he came an' asked for it. It seems he'd fallen on hard times. Ep Jackman held a mortgage on his hacienda an' lands an' he threatened to foreclose....'

'We jest found the mortgage,' said Hank.

'I never figured yuh would. Still, no matter now.... Don Miguel said that if I paid him back the money I owed him pronto he'd get in the clear with Jackman. But I couldn't give it to him. Ah hadn't got it. He went away in a rage and I didn't hear any more about it till a few days later. Then that young hellion of a son of his rode in with a proposition for me.' Withers paused. 'You're not gonna like this, boys,' he said. He continued. 'José said the old man was desperate. That he, the son, would do anything rather than the Carmenitos should lose their beloved hacienda. In fact, he had a plan whereby they could get out o' the woods. All they wanted was my assurance that Ah'd shut me eyes to anythin' that happened. Ah could pay my debt that way an' they'd keep their mouths shut. If I refused, wal, they'd ruin me.... I was a weak old fool. I agreed to do as they said.' He stopped, gasping for breath.... 'Come closer. Ah've got to hurry.'

Hank and Pete leaned nearer to him. He continued:

'When you came an' told me about ole Joe Dempsey I wasn't sure whether it wuz the Carmenitos' doin' or not. Ole Joe wuz a friend o' mine.... Then Clem was killed – an' Mackey (who'd bin told to get you) to make sure he didn't talk. Clem was like a son to me.... I rode over to the hacienda....

'Don Miguel said Clem had put up a fight and José had had to kill him. It was José and Le Bruque who did the job. José used the knife – he's a hellion – a cold-blooded young fiend. I threatened to expose them. In turn Don Miguel threatened to expose me. He said I was an accessory now – by exposing him Ah'd be exposing mahself too. I'd be disgraced – be hounded from the country. Ah'm an old man – Ah've nowhere tuh go.... Nothin' Ah could do would bring Clem back – or old Joe. I was weak – weak....

'They'd got old Joe's map, an' half of the claim. You had the other half. They wanted it. They asked me to get it for 'em. Ah liked you boys, Ah didn't know what to do. I sent those two men to your room. José didn't trust me so he followed them. They thought they'd got the claim. When José discovered it was only a rifle licence he went mad. You know what happened to Grip Scanlon.... He took a band of men and ole Joe's map an' went to look for the claim. They couldn't even find it.... Ole Joe was cute – his map was in cypher or somep'n. Ah guess only he could read it.'

'Take a shot of this,' said Hank. He held a flask to the dying man's lips. Withers drank. 'I can make it,' he said.

'... The Carmenitos were sunk. Their last chance was to kill Jackman before he foreclosed. Le Bruque was sent to do this. But he bungled it. Carlo saw him but was too scared to talk. He knew one of the mob 'ud get him sooner or later if he gave Le Bruque away. Wal, Le Bruque got him – jest like he got young Marty after the kid had spotted him an' José at the jail. If Marty had come into town an' spilled the beans instead o' runnin' away he might've bin alive now....

'Ah was gettin' to the end o' my tether. Ah wuz fightin' back a bit – as a last resource I meant to tell you boys everythin' an' tuh hell with the consequences....' He lapsed into mutterings. 'Weak.... weak.'

'Marshal,' Hank urged him. 'Marshal.'

Withers took another pull at the flask. 'All right,' he said. '... Ah guess the Carmenitos got busy this last coupla days. They sent Le Bruque here to get Carlo – an' me as well. I figured that; that's why Ah wanted tuh get Le Bruque first. Then Ah meant to tell you boys everythin'. Wal, he ain't beat me yet…. Probably José himself went to Sundown City to fix Jackman before he got to his lawyer…. Then with me out of the way, an' Carlo, an' Jackman, they'd be sittin' pretty – an' with plenty o' time to look for ole Joe's gold mine…. Too bad Le Bruque didn't shoot straighter, eh, boys.' Withers laughed weakly, then began to cough. He was almost done. He gasped. His voice was a whisper when he spoke again.

'Get – get Sam Fernicutt an' tell him…. He will help you get a posse…. Ride to the hacienda. Get them all.' He shuddered. His head fell back. His eyes closed. He died peacefully.

The bell jangled as Pete Henderson opened the door of Stella Dempsey's little draper's shop. Hardly had he closed it than feet pattered outside and it was swung open again. Blowzy, yellow-haired Biddy, Big Harry's woman, entered. She gave Pete a sullen look but did not speak.

Stella came through from the back. She looked surprised to see them both standing there. So late, too. She kept open late for the benefit of 'the girls.' 'Evening, Biddy,' said she. 'Evening, Pete.'

'Evenin',' the other two chorused. Then they glared at each other.

'See tuh the lady first, Stella,' said Pete.

Biddy said: 'I want a coupla yards o' that light blue ribbon.'

Stella got it for her and the dance-hall girl left. Before the door closed on her she gave a scornful toss of her head in the direction of Pete.

Again Stella looked surprised. Pete said: 'I had a run-in the other day with her fellah, Big Harry.'

'Oh,' said Stella. She smiled.

'What's the matter,' said Pete, cheekily. 'Jealous?'

Now it was Stella's turn to toss her head. 'I should think not!' Then she froze up, her lovely face a disdainful mask.

Pete grinned uncertainly. Why didn't he keep his mouth shut? 'I wuz jest kiddin',' he said.

Stella's face became sunny again. Pete figured maybe *she'd* only been kidding, too. She seemed to have a roguish sense of humour. She said: 'All right, Pete.'

His face sobered suddenly as he remembered fully the main thing that had brought him here. 'I've got some news for you, Stella,' he said.

The girl's face clouded, too, as she sensed his urgency and sadness.

He followed her through into the back place. It was the first time he had been in there. He liked what he saw. She drew a chair up before the glowing pot-bellied stove. He took off his hat and sat down.

The Indian girl came in from the kitchen. Stella asked her for coffee. She nodded and padded away, her moccasins making little sibilant sounds on the gaily coloured rush mats that were strewn on the floor.

Pete had an all-over impression of dark polished furniture, gleaming crockery and gaily coloured curtains. He began to tell Stella the story of Marshal Withers and the rest.

The girl's eyes widened as his story progressed. Then she dropped her head and her face was hidden. He could only see the smooth white line of her forehead and the scintillating cloud of her dark hair with russet glints in the lamp-light as she sat in the low basket-work chair in front of him.

When he had finished she still did not look up. Not until he spoke to her directly again. He leaned closer, irresistibly drawn by the charm of her in her shimmering white shirtwaist and tight brown skirt. At her throat was a small gold clasp. He said: 'It's pretty evident it was the Carmenitos, or a couple of their men, who killed your father....'

She fingered the little gold brooch as she looked up. Her eyes were bright with tears. She said: 'Yes ... but Marshal Withers? ... I can hardly believe it.'

''It's true all right, Stella.'

'Yes, I know, but it's still hard to believe. He was my father's friend.'

'He didn't have anything directly tuh do with any of it,' said Pete. 'He was jest a weak ole man.... He got in so deep he couldn't get out again. He wasn't really bad, Stella.'

'Oh, I'm sorry for him,' said Stella. 'He used to be so good to me. I'm sorry he had to be mixed up in it all. I feel no malice towards him.'

'Neither do I, I guess,' said Pete. Impulsively he reached forward and took her hand. She did not draw it away.

He said: 'We're riding to the Carmenito hacienda at dawn tomorrow. Everything'll be cleared up for good an' all then. I guess, figuring the marshal couldn't talk, they won't be expecting us.'

'Oh, Pete.' In her urgency she leaned towards him. He took both her hands. They were close together as she clung to him almost desperately. 'Does it have to be, Pete? There'll be more shooting – killings.'

'It's got to be, Stella. Don't you see? The Carmenitos have been at the bottom of everything. They must be stopped forever. They've been like a cancer on the territory for years. They've got to be removed....'

'Yes, I see.... You're going, Pete?'

'Yes, I'm going. You know that. You wouldn't want me to stay behind, would you?'

Her voice came to him in a pleading whisper: 'Look after yourself tomorrow, Pete....' Then, so softly that he only just heard it: 'For my sake.'

'I'll look after myself, *chiquita*,' he said.

Then words failed him, he caught hold of her chin and raised her face until she looked up at him. Her eyes were bright pools; bright with joy now, not tears.

He bent and kissed her.

While they were in this embrace, lost to the world, they did not hear the Indian girl enter again carrying coffee on a tray. The girl watched for a moment, her face inscrutable but her dark eyes glowing. Then she returned to the kitchen. Poco, her father, had just come in from the yard. In her own language she whispered to him of what she had seen.

'It is good,' said Poco in border dialect. 'The Pete *senore* is a good hombre.'

In the other room the lovers broke away. Stella looked around her dazedly then was pulled once more to Pete's broad chest. Her voice came muffled once more: 'I knew it all the time, Pete. I knew it … didn't you?'

'Yeh, honey, I guess I did.' He chuckled. 'An' I guess there ain't nothin' at all we can do about it.'

'Nothing at all,' she echoed.

'Yeh, looks like we're stuck all right,' Pete caressed her again. Then he said: 'I guess I'll hafta go now, honey. Hank's waiting for me.'

'I'll come out with you and lock up,' said the girl.

They went out hand in hand. There in the gloom of the shop as the girl turned the lamp out they kissed again.

'Look after yourself,' she whispered.

'I will, *chiquita*. Good-night.'

Her reply was a husky murmur. Another firm pressure of his hand. Then he was gone.

FOURTEEN

The panorama of San Diablo Creek was etched by the approaching dawn, like black cardboard scenery: craggy, mis-shapen against a grey back-cloth. A mournful little breeze, fugitive from the brooding hills, disturbed the dust as it wandered down Main Street. Lights flashed on in windows, pale yellow squares, sickly in the muddy grey light. Voices sounded, harsh in the stillness, as early risers called the sluggards from their beds. There was work to be done this day!

Then as the sky began to lighten, streaked with yellow and pale crimson, men began to appear on all sides. Many of them were buckling on their gun-belts as they came. They carried rifles and shotguns. They began to lead their horses out on to the street, to congregate in front of the San Diablo Palace. They greeted each other in mono-syllables.

It was a grim band of men that rode from San Diablo Creek that morning as dawn was breaking over the Western skies. They did not talk. They rode straight, swiftly, eating up the miles with steadily drumming hooves. They were fighting men all; outlaws many of them; not a one that had not, metaphorically speaking, got half-a-dozen or more notches on his guns. Their faces were alike in their cold masks of resolve. They had a mission to fulfil.

Hank McDonald, Pete Henderson and Sam Fernicutt rode at their head.

It was Hank who raised his arm in a sweeping forward movement as, after what seemed countless hours of incessant galloping, they saw the hacienda of Don Miguel Carmenito dimly through the shimmering haze that betokened there was a broiling day ahead.

They were at the outlying buildings before they were seen. They ran into a small bunch of vaqueros. One, more foolhardy than the rest, raised a rifle. He was shot from his horse. The rest fled, striving to reach the shelter of the stockade which surrounded the hacienda proper. Only two reached it, and they were not in time to shut the gates. The cavalcade swept in.

But the alarm had been given. People opened fire from the windows and innumerable loopholes of the hacienda. It was built like a fort and had withstood many an Indian raid.

'Take cover,' yelled Hank.

They did so, leaving four of their number lying on the cold slabs of the patio. They hid behind carts, behind barrels. A half-dozen of them led by Hank and Pete took cover in some disused stables.

'If we cut thru' here,' said Pete, 'maybe we can get behind the house – or at least get 'em on the flank.'

'It's worth trying,' said one of the men.

'Yeh,' said Hank. 'I figure they ain't got their full force here by the sound of the shootin'. I daresay there's a good many out on the mesa. They're not important anyway – we want the ring-leaders. We gotta work fast before they get properly organised. If any force does happen to come in, we'll be between two fires.'

He led the way through the stables and out of a back

door into a smaller patio. In front of them was a narrow side of the hacienda with one door and one window. Somebody opened up at them from the window as they ran across the yard. One of them fell, his face a bloody mass. Dropping on one knee Hank fanned his gun. Somebody screamed beyond the window. Then silence.

The five men threw themselves at the door. It gave way. Slugs whistled over their heads as they dived in. Hank's hat flew off. Another man rose too soon and shared the fate of the man in the yard. His face was not pretty, either.

The remaining four retaliated. A few scattered shots in return went wide.

'Rush 'em!' yelled Hank, bounding to his feet.

He fell head first over a body in the dark passage up which they sped. Shots rattled and one tore a groove in his shoulder. A man screamed behind him. Hank turned. 'Pete?'

'I'm all right,' said Pete. 'But now there's only three of us…. Quick, in here.' He pulled Hank and the other man through a door into a small room that looked like a study. A figure turned from the window, pistol levelled. Pete fired from the hip. The man fell, blood staining his white hair.

'An old man!' exclaimed Pete.

Hank turned him over. 'He's dead,' he said.

The third man, a red-headed gun-slinger who worked for Fernicutt, said: 'It's Don Miguel. The old skunk had it comin' to him.'

Hank looked down into the dark, aristocratic features grimacing in death. 'Yeh, I guess he did,' he said.

The red-head fired as a Mexican appeared in the door-way. The man fell backwards, his gun barking and sending its slug into the ceiling. The red-head ran to the door and strode over the body. He fired up the passage as Hank and Pete followed him.

'Another one,' he said. Then he whooped and ran on.

The partners heard a familiar voice.

'Fernicutt,' said Pete.

They ran after the red-head.

They joined him and Fernicutt at the bottom of the passage. They had to stride over two dead Mexicans on their way down.

Another dead man was sitting propped up against the wall beside Fernicutt. His mouth was wide open, his teeth bared in a hideous grimace, his eyes staring.

Fernicutt said: 'But we ain't got José, or Le Bruque, or the old man; they must've slipped out the back way.'

'We got the old man,' said Hank. 'But we haven't seen José or Le Bruque.'

'If we haven't got 'em we will,' said Pete. 'I'll get my hoss.' He ran. Hank followed him.

Pete, young, impetuous, took the trail first. But Hank was not far behind him.

The fugitives could only ride one way and that was to the border. And they had not got much start. Pete spurred his horse.

Ten minutes hard riding and he was rewarded by the sight of the quarry in a valley below him. They were getting out into the desert and scrub again now. They were not far from the border. Here and there outcrops of rock broke the arid monotony.

Even as he saw the riders ahead of him Pete became aware that his own horse was tiring. He cursed himself for not getting a fresh one from the hacienda. He spurred on, striving to keep the quarry in sight. He looked back and waved. Hank was catching up.

Then Lady Luck took a hand in the game. Pete saw one of the other men's mounts stumble.

Next moment both horse and rider were rolling in the dust. Faintly on the breeze Pete heard the man yell as he rose to his feet. The horse lay still. The other rider did not pause, he did not even seem to glance back. He kept his horse at a gallop. It was a big beast, jet-black. Pete reckoned the rider must be José. His actions were characteristic of his black soul.

The other man shook his fist after his erstwhile friend and ran for the cover of a nearby long outcrop of rocks. The horse lay where it had fallen. As he got nearer Pete saw its leg was broken. It had stumbled in a gopher hole. Pete drew his gun and put a slug in its brain as he passed.

Behind him Hank yelled: 'Watch yourself!'

He had not spoken too soon for, even as the echoes of his cry died away, from the rocks a gun boomed. A slug whipped Pete's hat off. He caught it on the cantle of his saddle.

He held his own fire, getting nearer, zig-zagging his horse so that he made a difficult target. By the sound of it he figured it was a Colt the other man had used. According to that he hadn't got a rifle – which was a good thing for his pursuers.

Riding hard, Hank caught up. The Colt boomed again. It was a long shot but it found a mark. Hank's horse skidded to a stop, a convulsive shudder ran through its frame. Hank threw himself clear as the wounded beast pitched over on its side. It snorted. Its eyes rolled convulsively. Then they became glassy, the heaving body became still. Shot through the breast, the beast was dead.

Hank got up, cursing, running with his gun in his hand.

'It's Le Bruque, I think,' he said.

'I'll handle him,' said Hank. 'Get after the other one.'

'Hank....'

'Do as I say,' snarled the old-timer. He kept on running. The man in the rocks fired again. The slug buzzed between the two men.

'I'll cover yuh,' said Pete. He wheeled his horse again.

He raised his gun and fired at the rocks where Le Bruque was hidden.

Hank followed, both guns out now. He made for the cover of a huge boulder at one end of the long outcrop. Le Bruque was ensconced somewhere the other end. Pete's shooting made him keep his head down, giving Hank the chance he sought. He made one last desperate spurt and flung himself flat behind the boulder.

'Keep goin',' he yelled. Pete kept going.

'Now then, my fancy-shirted friend,' growled Hank. 'Yuh can't creep around behind doors now. You've got to stay an' shoot it out.'

Unhurriedly, he eased himself into a more comfortable position. He checked his guns. Then he took off his hat, put it on a gun-barrel and stuck it up so that the crown showed above the top of the rock.

The other man's gun boomed. Hank jerked the hat down.

He grinned mirthlessly and tossed the Stetson in the air. The Colt boomed again. Hank rose swiftly, firing himself. He saw Le Bruque's head for a minute, then the man bobbed down again. Whether he had hit him or not Hank did not know. He soon found out as two more slugs came perilously close. Hank hugged cover. 'Keep on shootin', pardner,' he said. 'Your ammunition won't last for ever.'

He changed his position. He lay flat on his stomach. Then methodically he began to dig in the soft sand with one hand. He dug at the base of the rock. He started at the end, his hand working in the open, unnoticed by the other, then working right along the base of the boulder. In a few seconds he had worked a trench deep enough to take his lean body as he lay flat. The head of it was out in the open.

There was no sound from the other man. He was waiting, too. Maybe he thought his opponent had been hit. Maybe he was crawling nearer.

Hank rolled and lay on his back in the shallow trench.

He held his hat on the barrel of his left-hand gun. The other gun was ready in his hand. As he lay flat his head was away from the boulder but hidden in the trench.

Hank had been an Indian fighter; he knew all the tricks. Now he was all set.

He elevated his hat again on the gun barrel. He raised the crown of it above the boulder.

Up ahead Le Bruque's Colt boomed. He missed. Hank raised his head a little from the trench. He was out of the line of fire. The hat jumped as the other fired again. Then Hank got a glimpse of that fancy shirt and opened up.

Hit in the chest Le Bruque spun out of cover, rolled on his belly. For a moment his glaring eyes, dreadful in surprise, looked into the icy ones of the old fighter. Then Hank fired twice. Little puffs of dust started from Le Bruque's clothing. Then he rolled again, on to his face, and lay still.

The pace of Pete's horse was beginning to flag sadly. The cowboy figured he'd never catch up with José at this rate. The Mexican's black stallion sure could travel. He was drawing steadily ahead.

José looked back. Then he seemed to slow down a little. His arm rose. There was a spurt of flame. A slug kicked up the sand in front of Pete's horse.

Now there was only one man following him José had evidently decided to fight, to get rid of the irritating encumbrance for ever. It was typical of his arrogance.

Pete fired back. The range was a bit too long for his Colt – although he had the advantage he did not have to turn in the saddle. The Mexican swivelled again. He fired. The slug bit into the ground almost at the feet of Pete's mount. The nag faltered, snorting in terror. Pete gentled him with his hands on the smooth neck. José fired again. The slug was losing its power as it bedded down at the side of Pete's horse.

Leaning forward over his neck, murmuring in his ear, Pete urged the beast forward. José was drawing in and getting the range now. He was getting mighty dangerous. As he turned again Pete raised his own Colt. They fired simultaneously. José's slug kicked up the dust beneath the belly of Pete's horse. The cowboy didn't know what had happened to his own shot. He certainly hadn't hit anything. He was busy now quietening his plunging beast. Gentled down, the horse loped on again. But it had done some travelling today and was noticeably weaker. José was drawing away again.

Pete's mouth set in a rigid line, the muscles bunching at the corners giving his face a drawn, almost cadaverous look. His eyes narrowed to wicked slits. He reached down to the long boot-sheath against his saddle and drew forth his rifle.

He raised the Winchester to his shoulder, balancing himself upright in the saddle with a grip of his knees to the horse's flanks.

As Pete sighted the rifle, José turned in the saddle again. Pete squeezed the trigger.

The crash of the rifle awakened fiendish echoes in these desolate, sun-tortured places. The powder-smoke drifted in a blue haze before Pete's face, then was wafted away.

He saw José's black stallion swerving, prancing. Then going on again. Its rider hanging low on its neck.

Pete raised the Winchester again, his mouth was a vicious line as he squinted deliberately. He squeezed the trigger once more. The report battled on his eardrums.

Through the smoke haze he saw José's horse buckle and go down. The rider was thrown clear, stooping, running for the cover of the rocks.

Pete felt a twinge of regret. The four-legged critturs were certainly catching out on this trip. That he had hit that magnificent beast instead of the skunk that rode it made him burn with rage. He fired again as José scrambled for cover. He cursed. The slug had kicked up dust at the Mexican's heels.

Then José was in cover. He fired back; Pete heard the whine of the bullet. He sheathed his rifle, drew his Colt again and retaliated with that.

Another shot followed directly on his own. A slug whipped Pete's hat off.

Pete flung himself from his horse. He rolled. Another slug missed him by yards. Pete rose, lunged forward. He fired as he ran, weaving and bobbing. Then he tried an old trick. As another slug came perilously close, he crumpled, then lay still on his side.

José came from behind a rock, his gun raised for a finishing shot. Pete beat him to it. His slug took the Mexican plumb in the chest, spinning him round. He regained his balance and came on like a madman, his eyes glaring, his teeth bared in a horrible snarl.

Pete rose on one knee, firing coolly. José did not have time to get his gun in line again. It fell from his lax fingers as he crumpled up. He fell forward on his face and lay still.

Pete rose slowly to his feet. He turned. Hank was coming across the desert towards him.

'You all right, younker?'

'Shore, Hank. You?'

'Yeh.'

'How about Le Bruque?'

'Buzzard bait,' said the oldster laconically. 'An amateur badman.'

'Odds on this buzzard,' said Pete, indicating the crumpled form of José Carmenito. 'He nearly cashed me in for keeps.'

'Wal,' said Hank. 'He won't do no more hell-raisin' now.'

They went over to the body together.

'Look, Hank,' said Pete. 'His spurs.'

They were fancy Mexican rowels, the star type. Pete went down on his knees.

'Yeh, this one's got a spike missin' all right,' he said.

He took the little glistening spike from his vest pocket.

'It all started when we found this,' he said. 'Let it end with this.'

He let the little glittering piece of metal fall from his hand. It was swallowed up in the dust beside the body. Pete rose to his feet.

It was late afternoon when the silent band of fighting men returned to Diablo, bringing their wounded and their dead with them. The darkling skies were suffused with crimson; the air was hotter than ever, brooding and still. A storm was in the offing. It was badly needed in Diablo to sweeten the air, to wash away filth and dust, and the odour of blood and battle that the returning men brought with them. Maybe in some measure it was needed to wash away the evil that had stagnated like a hidden cesspool there for so long – now that the main causes of that evil had been destroyed for ever.

As the weary, bloodied fighting men entered the Main Street and passed the little draper's shop there, a wild-haired girl ran out calling: 'Pete! Pete!'

'Stella,' a voice answered her.

She ran to the side of him and clung to his stirrup. 'Oh, I'm so glad you're safe. So glad....'

Sam Fernicutt smiled a little wistfully. Beside him Hank McDonald's eyes widened. Then he smiled, too. The smile reached his eyes this time, lighting them up with a glow such as had not been there for many, many years.

EPILOGUE

The years were kind to San Diablo Creek, 'The Devil's Frying Pan' of ballad and fable. The hills took away their curse and opened their heart once more. Again the waters ran with wealth and in the fringe of the hills beside the creek was born the Dempsey-Henderson Mine, which gave an honest living to hundreds of people from all corners of the States.

Diablo was booming again and it meant to stay that way – before it the mine, behind it the ever-growing ranches. It had its own town hall and bank and theatre, and Sam Fernicutt's Saloon and Emporium was the finest in the State. There was a huge dance hall, too, as well as dozens of smaller honky-tonks. It was no namby-pamby set-up; it was still a rough, boisterous Western town.

But its vice was cut to a minimum, and any hoodlum or owl-hooter who didn't like that set-up could settle things with the marshal, a hardbitten, quick-shooting old-timer named Hank McDonald. His deputy, Pete Henderson, was also a big noise at the mines – married to the owner they said, and a danged pretty girl she was to boot.

They had a son, two years old and named after his grandfather, Joe Dempsey, who was one of the founders of Diablo and the cause of the bonanza that brought about its rebirth.

Young Joe certainly had a lot to be proud and thankful for – a glorious heritage ... and an exciting, glittering future before him.